BY LIZZIE

BY LIZZIE

{ Mary Eccles }

Dial Books for Young Readers
New York

Published by Dial Books for Young Readers

A division of Penguin Putnam Inc.

345 Hudson Street

New York, New York 10014

Designed by Lily Malcom

Text set in Garamond

Printed in the U.S.A. on acid-free paper

1 3 5 7 9 10 8 6 4 2

Library of Congress Cataloging-in-Publication Data

Eccles, Mary, date.

By Lizzie / Mary Eccles.

p. cm.

Summary: Lizzie, the middle child of divorced parents, uses her mother's
old typewriter to record the events in her life the year before she turns ten.

ISBN 0-8037-2608-2

[1. Family life—Wisconsin—Fiction. 2. Schools—Fiction.

3. Authorship—Fiction. 4. Wisconsin—Fiction.] I. Title.

PZ7.E1963 By 2001

[Fic]—dc21 00-030337

For Claire and Nora

✴ CONTENTS ✴

BY LIZZIE

THE TYPEWRITER
* * *

JANUARY

Click, clack.

Stuffed in the closet, the beat-up metal case with the peeling stickers looks like a piece of junk. It's not what I'm looking for, either.

When I find Winston's leash, we're supposed to go for a walk in the snow. "Take your boots, Lizzie," Mom calls from the window. "It's still coming down."

This walk is supposed to cheer me up. It's January 1, the day after my birthday, and I'm in a bad mood. I just turned nine, and I had a nice party. Vanilla cake with butterscotch frosting, helium balloons, and a new board game that Mom "saved" from Christmas. But now it's over, and my next birthday—my tenth—is a whole year away.

The last day of December is a lousy time for a birthday, if you ask me. After Christmas, after every other holiday and everybody else's birthday, along comes mine. "Tough luck, Lizzie," says Norman, my brother. "You blew it! Last-one-in-the-family-to-have-a-birthday-is-a-rotten . . ."

"I'm not listening!" I shout, to drown out the last word. Besides, in our family, I'm not really last—except for my birth date. I'm in between Norman, who's twelve, and Ellie, who's two. Winston is six in people years, so he's right there in the middle—with me. But, then again, that's older than all of us in dog years. Even Mom!

I drag the case with the peeling stickers out of the closet. My boots are in back, along with the leash. But I stop in the hall to read the stickers. France, Greece, Brazil, Australia. The rest are smudged or torn off.

I find Mom on the floor of the living room, playing with Ellie. "Here goes the doggie, and here comes the mouse." Mom wiggles two finger puppets at Ellie. I push the case into her lap.

"Gracious, my typewriter!" Mom snaps the lid open. Inside, it looks like our computer, with keys for each letter of the alphabet. The numbers and punctuation marks have their own keys, too. Everything's coated with dust. "Whew," says Mom, stopping a sneeze. "I haven't used *this* in a while."

"Can I try it?" I ask. "I know how to type, if I look at the keys."

Mom sets up the typewriter on a card table. She shows me the long metal bar, which turns the roller to start a new line.

Click, clack. Right away, I love that sound. Our computer only whirs.

"How come it has all these stickers?" I ask.

"I took it all around the world," Mom says. "On a great big trip, before you were born."

Mom explains how one year, after college, she wanted to travel. "I didn't know what to do with myself, and I hadn't saved up much money. This typewriter paid for the trip."

"How?" I'm stumped, since Mom didn't sell the thing.

"I wrote stories," she says, "in each country I went to." Her hometown newspaper published every single one. "My first real job." She smiles. "Funny how one thing led to another." Mom still works for that newspaper.

I touch the stickers. "What did you write about in all of these places?" I ask. "Was it hard to find things?"

"Not really," she says. "Writing stories helped me know the countries better and find my way around. I had an excuse to poke around and talk to people. And soon a new place wasn't unfamiliar anymore." She put her hand on my shoulder. "Sometimes the people I met *were* my story. Wherever you go, you meet somebody interesting."

Click, clack, click-click, clack-clack. I type **LIZZIE** on a piece of paper. Who do I know who's interesting?

"Uh-oh." There's Ellie, climbing on my lap. "You can watch," I say. "But don't touch."

Ellie puts her fingers on the keys. "Mine."

"Nope." I push her hands out of my way. *Clicka, clicka, clicka*: I press the backspace key. In front of **LIZZIE**, I type **BY**. *Click-clack.*

"Since you're busy," Mom says, "I'll take Winston out." But Winston has other ideas. When Mom whistles, he bounds in—right past her. After giving Ellie a sniff, Winston sticks his head in my lap.

"Come on, Winston. It's getting crowded. Weren't you going for a walk?" I stop typing for a second to stroke Winston's fur. His ears point up like triangles.

JKLJKL. Ellie is typing—on *my* page—with one finger. "Get off," I shout, "or I'm getting Mom."

But Mom takes Winston out, not Ellie. Worse yet, Norman barges in.

"What are you doing with that old thing?" he asks. *Click, clack, clack-clack, click.*

Ellie slides off, to play with the stickers on the typewriter case. Norman just stands there.

"So what are you writing about?"

Anybody but Norman would see I'm too busy to answer.

"'I found Mom's typewriter,'" he reads over my shoulder.

"'It's very old and dusty. It went on a trip around the world.'" Norman stops to snicker. "Wow, Lizzie. Now that's fascinating." He pinches my shoulder. "I can't wait to read more."

I slap my hand over the page. "Go away. You're bothering me."

Norman fakes a hurt look. "All I said was, 'Wow! Fascinating!' What comes next?"

I chew on the end of one of my braids. Mom says she chews gum when she writes her newspaper stories. When she's on a deadline, she says the chewing helps her concentrate.

"Let's see," I say. "In the next part, the big brother, who's also a big pest, goes bye-bye."

From the floor, Ellie giggles. "Pig pest go bye-bye."

Norman pokes Ellie. "Takes one to know one." To me he mutters, "I have better things to do than watch you pretend you're Mom!"

Norman stomps off quickly. He always has to have the last word. But as soon as I turn my head, to stick out my tongue at him, Ellie climbs right back up. *Click click click, click click click.* JKLJKL.

"Oh, look what you did." I groan and pull out the paper. "Let's find your crayons." I give Ellie the paper to color on, but first I cross out my name.

I carry the typewriter over to the window seat, my favorite

place in our house. I kick off my shoes so I can sit cross-legged, with the typewriter on my lap. The typewriter doesn't feel heavy or clunky. If it did, Mom couldn't have taken it so many places, I guess.

Outside, Winston leads Mom through the snow. They stop at the creek at the edge of our yard. I'm not pretending, not the way Norman meant. But I like tapping these keys that have been around the world.

I roll in a new sheet of paper and start over. **BY LIZZIE**. *Click, click, clack, clack, click, clack, click, clack.* I can't go away on a trip, the way Mom did. But with the very same typewriter, I will write fascinating stories of my own. In a year, when I'm ten, we'll see what I've done.

Norman is back again. "Finished yet?"

"Oh no," I say, pulling out my first typed page.

I'm just beginning.

NO FAIR!
* * *

FEBRUARY

I'd rather be in Arizona.

For a short month, this one drags. Not for Norman, who has his birthday to look forward to. (Or for Ellie, who doesn't know one month from another yet.)

But for me, the quicker February is over, the better. *I'm* not looking forward to Norman's birthday. Not at all. He'll be thirteen, in just a few days. He—and Mom—are excited about it. I bet some sort of surprise is planned.

Clickclickclickety-clicketyclackclackclack. I type faster now than I did when I first found Mom's typewriter. I don't always have to look down at the keys. Today I sit on the window seat, typing and watching it snow.

Where we live, in Wisconsin, we get lots of snow. This morning our yard is bright white. The bushes are covered with big white clumps, and ice sparkles on the bare branches of the trees.

Plunk! A snowball hits just under the window. Norman skids past. His nose is as red as Rudolph the reindeer's. Next comes Winston, chased by a sheepdog belonging to Norman's friend Chip. Soon all their tracks will crisscross the yard, spoiling that nice smooth ocean of snow.

Plink, plink. Two snowballs hit the window. I bang on it, but Norman ducks out of sight.

He turns up, seconds later, throwing the back door wide open. Winston stops on the doormat to shake snow off his fur. (I've trained him to do that!) The sheepdog trails Norman and Chip to the kitchen, dripping slush on the floor.

Norman scoops peppermint ice cream (my favorite flavor) into two dishes. Though I don't want any this minute (too cold!), I don't want Norman and Chip to finish it, either.

"Hello," I say. They ignore me. I peer into the half-gallon container, to see what's left.

"Lizard, do you mind?" Guarding the container, Norman elbows me away.

Lizard. Only Norman calls me that, because he knows I hate it. I wish I had a creepy-crawly-disgusting nickname for him, too. Maybe while I'm staring at the typewriter keys, I'll come up with one.

Chip sneezes into his hand, then licks his fingers. "Yuck," I say, under my breath.

The sheepdog climbs on Chip's lap. Norman pulls out the sports page of the newspaper to show Chip. The minute Chip's head is turned, his dog sticks his nose in the ice cream dish. "Somebody stop him!" I shout.

"Stop what?" Norman growls. Chip's dish is licked clean, but they don't care! The sheepdog jumps down, tongue hanging out, telltale pink droplets on his hair. As he bounds off to huddle with Winston, I make a yuck-face. Nobody sees me.

Chip blows his nose in a napkin. He sounds just like a goose. I stand behind him, stretching my neck and flapping my arms. When Norman looks up from his ice cream, I duck!

Norman helps himself to more. At least he uses the scoop. Chip sticks his spoon in and eats from the container.

I scrunch up my face—I can't help it. "You might leave some for the rest of us."

Norman shoves the container in my face. "Have it all, Miss Piggy. Eat the whole thing while I'm gone."

Gone? "Where are you going?"

Norman sniffs. "Wouldn't you like to know."

While Norman waits for me to ask him again, Chip says, "Man, did you luck out. Get me some autographs while you're at it."

That's how I hear about Norman going to Arizona, for five days, with Dad. It's a baseball trip—timed so they'll see the Milwaukee Brewers at spring training.

"Their rookie pitcher's the guy to watch," says Norman.

"Yeah," says Chip, stopping another sneeze. "Soak up some rays, take a side trip to the Grand Canyon. . . ."

What? My mouth hangs open, but no sound comes out. My best friend, Carol, went to the Grand Canyon last Christmas. She showed me the most fantastic photographs of it. I'm dying to go.

While Norman and Chip talk baseball—how so-and-so's going to have his best season ever—I slip out of the kitchen. No fair! No fair! I stamp my feet all the way up the stairs. I have to find Mom, to ask why this is happening. No way I can ask Dad.

Dad doesn't live with us. The year after Ellie was born, Dad and Mom got divorced. Then Dad moved to Minnesota. He's taken Norman and me on car trips to his house, about five hours away, and he comes back here for visits every other month. But nobody's taken a special trip with Dad to a faraway place. Until now.

I charge into my room (which I share with Ellie). Mom, hemming a skirt, points to Ellie napping and puts a finger to her lips.

I will *not* be hushed. "How come Norman gets to go to Arizona?"

"It's his birthday present," Mom whispers.

"I had a birthday, and nobody took me to Arizona." As my voice rises, Mom drops her sewing and leads me out to the hall.

"Lizzie, listen, this is about baseball. They're going to training camp, to watch the Brewers—"

"So? I like baseball, too. And what if they go to the Grand Canyon?"

"The Grand Canyon?" Mom repeats. "I don't think so. But I don't know exactly what your father has in mind these days." She reaches over to stroke my hair. "I'm sorry, Lizzie. But that's the plan, for Norman and your father to go together. Try to understand."

I pull away so fast that my hair hurts. "I *don't* understand. Why can't I go? Why am I *always* the one left out?"

"Lizzie, stop arguing with me. It's your father's present to Norman. When you're older, and can take an airplane flight by yourself, I'm sure your father—"

When you're older. That does it. I stomp off down the stairs.

The typewriter table gets a big shove as I slump on my window seat. *Click, click, click, bang.* I slam my hand on the space bar. I'm stuck—stuck in the middle of this family. If I were the oldest, I'd get to go on a big, special trip. If I were the baby, I wouldn't care.

NofairnofairnofairnofairnofairnofairNOFAIR!

I feel better writing that down. I fill a whole page with nofairs and rip it out. Winston's ears point up when he hears the noise. I toss him the paper, crumpled into a ball.

As Chip and the sheepdog leave through the back door, a chilly gust of wind pushes its way inside. "Have fun in the sun," Chip calls out as my teeth chatter. "Remember my autographs."

The door slams. Norman whistles to Winston, retrieving my wadded-up paper from his mouth.

"What's no fair?" he asks, and gets no answer from me.

Winston follows him over, panting and drooling. Norman uses my paper to wipe Winston's mouth.

This time, Norman sees my yuck-face. "What's wrong with you, Lizard? You're such a crab."

"Don't call me Lizard. And I'm not a crab."

"My mistake. You're sulky . . . and rude."

"Oh, leave me alone." My face feels hot. I give the typewriter table another kick.

Norman re-crumples my paper and tosses it into my lap.

"When are you leaving?" I ask.

"When I feel like it. You don't own the living room."

"I mean, leaving for Arizona." The word sticks in my throat. When I stare at the typewriter, the keys blur.

"So that's why you're mopey," Norman says. "You're going to miss me?" Whistling to Winston, he goes out.

Clickclickclick-ping! Why didn't I think of *that* before? While Norman's away with Dad, I'll have five whole days without Norman! In the nine years I've been in this family, I'll bet *that's* never happened.

I decide to type up a list of all the things I can do with Mom. I add an *E* next to those we could do with Ellie—and a *B,* for baby-sitter, next to the rest. (I count to make sure there are more B's than E's.)

```
Ice-skating B
Sledding/park E
Sledding/big hill by the high school B
Baking angel food cake from scratch E
A Disney movie about animals E
A scary late-night movie B
Bowling/duck pins E
Bowling/real pins B
Spring clothes shopping in Milwaukee B
Indoor picnic E
```

I look up and around. No Norman. He's still outside throwing snowballs for Winston to chase. Now I can't wait for his trip. While he's gone, I'll be the oldest. For five great days.

"Super," Mom says when she sees my list. "Let's do them

all." Right away she calls up our cousin Lucy to baby-sit. On the list, we write down movies we want to see, new places to try for lunch. Mom jots down her own ideas, too: a special tour of her office, so I can see the newspaper printed; a café with make-your-own sundaes to try for lunch. She also says if I'd like Carol to sleep over one night, we can have Norman's room. I say "super" to all!

We draw up menus for suppers at home. I plan an "indoor picnic" on a blanket in front of our fireplace. Mom promises pepperoni pizza, with dough made from scratch. My offer is homemade hot cocoa, with marshmallows roasted over the fire.

On the morning of his trip, Norman coughs. *Hack, hack, hackedy, hack.* The noise wakes Ellie and me at the other end of the hall.

"Just a cold," he tells Mom. "Probably caught it from Chip." But as soon as he tries to get out of bed, he has to lie down. Mom takes Norman's temperature: 103 degrees. His head and his chest hurt, too.

Our doctor checks Norman. It's a bad case of flu. Mom calls up Dad. The trip is called off.

At first Norman feels too sick to care. Mom lets him sleep, waking him every few hours for juice drinks and medicine. Mom says she'll rent some movies to watch, but otherwise we have to stay home.

All our plans, down the drain.

Dad sends Norman a baseball book and makes plans to visit. But they can't get to Arizona in time for spring training. Maybe, Dad says, he can come to Milwaukee for Opening Day of the baseball season. He'll try to get tickets to the Brewers game.

In time for his birthday, Norman's fever goes away. He sits in the living room, reading the sports page. He shows Mom a story on the Brewers' training camp. "We would have been there," he mutters, staring out a window at snow. "No fair."

"Surprise," Mom says, and hands me a blanket to spread in front of the fireplace. I dash to the kitchen to make cocoa and sample the marshmallows I'm going to roast. Mom's blueberry muffins, fresh from the oven, smell better than a birthday cake! I'll give the biggest muffin to Norman, with a candle in the middle (and some peppermint ice cream on the side).

Maybe next month will be fairer—to everybody.

Aaa-choo! Uh-oh.

EVEN THE DOG SWIMS
BETTER THAN I DO
* * *

MARCH

Swimming is stupid unless you're a fish.

Mom's done it again. I'm signed up for another round of
water torture. Every Saturday morning for the rest of the
winter is ruined! She could have asked me. I would have
said no.

"Do your best, Lizzie," says Mom, as if I'm the Little
Engine That Could. But I know I can't. My first new lesson is just like all the other times. I'm the worst swimmer
in the entire class.

"Jump in! Get wet!" the teacher shouts.

Everyone else plunges in, cannonball style. I slide in
slowly, feet first.

Everyone else kicks halfway across the pool. I kick
holding on to the side.

Everyone else floats. I sink the minute the teacher lets go of me.

Everyone else does handstands in the shallow end. I want to go home and play with Winston in my own backyard.

Marvin, the biggest boy in the class, splashes me. He blows bubbles and sprays water all over me, like a whale.

Norman swims in the advanced class at the deep end. He climbs onto the diving board. He waves to Mom, takes a running jump, and somersaults into the pool.

I hope I'll miss my turn. Maybe the teacher won't notice I'm here. Nobody else in my group is nine years old—not even close. It looks like I'll be a beginner forever, the oldest one on record!

"Michele, it's your turn," the teacher calls to me, even though my name is Lizzie. I correct her, but she keeps getting mixed up. She says I remind her of a girl named Michele in some other swimming class. Michele never jumps in the water, either.

"Everybody, blow bubbles," the teacher orders. "You, too, Michele."

I pretend I don't hear her. The last time I blew bubbles, I got water in my nose.

"Michele, do something!"

When will she learn I am *not* Michele?

Marvin and the others blow bubbles. The water turns

foamy and fizzy from all of that bobbing up and down. I count goose bumps on my arms. Forty-eight, forty-nine, fifty—I give up!

Then I watch the clock. The hands are not moving. What if the clock is broken and class never ends?

Norman climbs the high dive. He does a back flip—straight in, without a splash.

Finally, the class is over.

On the walk home, Norman brags. "My backstroke is the fastest in the class. And wasn't my last dive awesome?"

"Great," says Mom.

I shrug. "Not bad."

"Not bad?" Norman pokes me. "Did you jump in the pool today? How many times?"

"None of your business," I say.

"The answer is none. Zero."

If he ever does a belly flop, I hope I'm watching.

Mom pulls Norman aside. "Be fair. Swimming takes practice."

"Who needs practice to jump in the water?" Norman sneers. "When I was nine, I swam laps."

At home, I follow Winston into our backyard. The snow melted last week, and crocuses peek out from the muddy ground. Winston and I find sticks to collect.

Mom follows me. "Don't mind Norman," she says, putting an arm around me. "Learning to swim isn't easy."

"Now you tell me," I groan. "What if I just can't do it? Was swimming as hard for you as it is for me?"

Mom says, "At first I wouldn't go near the water, even though we lived by a lake. I had all kinds of excuses. Too cold. Too wavy. Too pebbly. Too fishy."

"How did you learn then?"

"My older brother taught me one summer. He promised to take me sailing once I learned to swim. I practiced like mad—in the lake, even in the bathtub."

After Mom goes inside, I sit on a tree stump and let Winston lick my hand. Mom was lucky—she had Uncle Steve for a brother. If he lived here, he could teach me to swim. He lives far away, though. In Seattle, near the ocean.

But what about Norman? He knows how to swim. So what if he shows off? He could help me—it can't hurt to ask him. At least he won't call me Michele.

"Teach you to swim?" Norman snorts. "Ha. I'd rather teach Winston!"

"Forget it," I say, but Norman doesn't.

"Come on, Winston!" Norman grabs one of my sticks. "Show Lizard how." (*Michele* doesn't seem so bad just now.)

Clickclickclackclack. Winston chases Norman to the creek. As Norman tosses the stick, Winston jumps in. Winston bobs up in a pool of bubbles and heads straight for the stick. His dog paddle is awesome.

Even the dog swims better than I do. But not for long, I promise myself.

Each day I practice—in the bathtub. I lie on my stomach in maybe four inches of water, and I hold my breath. In goes my face, halfway at first. I blow a few bubbles. Winston sits on the bath mat and keeps me company.

Soon, I'm adding more water and blowing more bubbles. Winston puts his front paws on the tub and licks my wet face. Maybe, if I pretend the pool is a great big bathtub, I'll be able to swim.

At the next lesson, I think I'm ready.

"Jump in!" the teacher shouts.

Splash! But not from me. I watch Marvin kick up a huge trail of foam. I dip my feet in the pool.

"Michele," calls the teacher. "Get wet!"

I am *not Michele!* I want to scream.

But somebody else cries out, "No, I can't." Right behind me, another girl huddles under her towel.

I slip off the edge of the pool. Ooo, the water's cold—freezing compared to my bathtub! Get used to it, I tell myself. Legs first, then arms. I think about Winston watching me from the bath mat, and I'm warmer already.

Holding on with one hand, I go under the water. I pop up, like a jack-in-the-box. I see the real Michele still sitting on the side. She must have come to our group to make up a class she missed.

She frowns at the teacher. "I want to go home."

"So did I. Last week I couldn't swim at all," I tell Michele. "But it gets easier. Come in with me."

"No." Michele hugs her knees. "It won't."

I lean back in the water and glide away from the side, pushing off with my feet. I'm floating! I don't sink, even when Marvin splashes by.

"Bravo!" says the teacher. "Soon you'll be swimming like a seal!"

I wonder if that means next time she'll know my name.

After each lesson I like swimming a little bit better. Michele hasn't come back to my class—maybe she gave up. But I'm glad I didn't, and I try something new in the water each time I go. Nobody has to drag me to the pool anymore.

Even Norman notices. "From up there on the high dive—just before I did that fabulous flip with a twist—I saw somebody who looked like you, Lizzie. Except this person did something that looked like a handstand."

"Wasn't it awesome?" I say on the walk back home. *Clickclickclick.* I skip to catch up with Mom and Ellie.

"Not bad," Norman calls after me. "Now I could show you a thing or two."

"Forget it." I turn and grin. "I don't need your help. You'll have to wait 'til Ellie's old enough for lessons. Or try to teach *Winston* to swim like *me!*"

Mom, was Uncle Steve a big show-off like you-know-who?

SLEEPOVER
* * *

April

Some guests are no fun at all.

Br-ringg! Carol phones me. "Lizzie, big problem! Can you do us a favor?"

"Like what?"

"Lizzie, best friends don't ask *what*. They *do* the favor. I'd do anything—I'd run to the rescue, if you had an emergency."

"Okay, I'll do it." I'm running in place. *Clickclickclick.* "Now tell me. What is it?"

It is a chicken. It's at Carol's house for an overnight visit because her little brother, Drew, brought it home from his kindergarten class. I think he's too young to take care of a chick that hatched in an incubator only ten days ago, but that's not the emergency.

"Dad is allergic to chickens," says Carol. "Drew let it

out of its cage and got feathers all over the place." Through the phone I hear sneezing. "Dad is a mess," she whispers. "The chick can't stay here!"

Explaining the chicken emergency to Mom, I promise, "I'll take care of it. Okay?"

"I don't know, Lizzie," says Mom, with a glance at the clock. She's working at home tonight, with a feature story to finish.

"But, Mom, it has nowhere else to go!"

"All right. As a favor to the Bradleys, it can come. But I hope you know what you're doing. I can't be much help."

I don't need help. If kindergarten kids like Drew are supposed to take care of a chicken, so can I!

Clickedy-click. I'm off to Carol's house, to rescue the chicken. She's outside waiting and springs up to greet me with a cage in her hand.

Carol says, "It's cute and fluffy." A towel hangs over the cage, so I can't see for myself. "Keep it covered," she advises, "so the chick won't get frightened while you're walking."

Waving my free hand, I turn to go home. Carol keeps shouting instructions—refill its food and water, clean out the cage. "Once should do it for the night," she says.

"Will do," I call back. "We'll get along fine."

"It loves to be cuddled," she calls after us. "It loves to play!"

At home, I remove the towel with a playful toss. The chicken is *not* as fluffy as I was expecting. Its feathers are dampish—the plastic water dish must have tipped over during our walk. And aren't most baby chicks yellow? This one is brownish-gray.

The chick shakes itself. *Cheep-cheep-cheep.*

"Hello, I'm Lizzie." I feel silly talking to a chicken. At least nobody else is listening.

Chee-ee-eep. That sound hurts my ears!

The chick hobbles about on toothpick-thin legs. It pecks at the newspaper on the tray of its cage.

"Are you hungry?" I see that its grain has spilled. "Just a second."

I move the typewriter to make room for the cage on the card table. The chick chirps again.

"Okay. I didn't forget you. Ready, set, here we go." As I lift the cage to the card table, the tray on the bottom slips out and clatters to the floor. "Uh-oh." I worry the chick fell out, too, but it must have seen this coming. It's climbing up one side of the cage, like a jungle gym.

I slam the cage on the table. *Chee-chee-chee-cheep!* The chick sticks its beak between the bars, but it can't get out.

"Hey, Lizzie, what's the racket?" Norman strolls over, peers into the cage. "What's this?"

"A chicken."

"No kidding." Norman sticks his finger in the cage.

The chicken jumps, banging into the side of the cage as it tries to flap its wings.

"Stop that!" I say to Norman. "You're scaring it!"

"You're not scared, are you?" Norman wiggles a finger outside the cage. The chicken seems to be watching.

"You're making it dizzy!"

"Lizzie, you're dizzy!" Norman laughs. "So what's it doing here?"

"Just visiting," I say. It feels like the chicken's been here a long time already. I wonder how long it "visited" Carol's family before she called me. *It loves to be cuddled . . . it loves to play.* Play? Here at our house, the chick paces and climbs the walls of its cage. I don't know what Carol was talking about.

Still twirling his finger, Norman says, "Have fun, you two." He strolls out.

The chicken huddles in the corner of the cage. Oops. I've forgotten to slide in the tray. Something drops from the chicken onto the card table. I see the same "stuff" on the floor near the tray.

"You need a diaper," I groan. "Maybe Ellie has a spare!"

I find cleaning supplies in the closet and begin to tackle the mess. First the floor, then the tray. *Chee-eep.* "Oh, shush!" I rap the table with the dustpan. *Clack.*

The chicken wanders around the cage, paying no attention to me. I find a section of newspaper near the magazine rack. I check its date—not today's. I fold the paper to put in the tray.

Uh-oh—we have company: Winston and Ellie. Winston sniffs the cage.

"No!" I shout. *Cheeeeeee!* A whirling puffball bangs about the cage—shrieking its head off. Winston sticks up his ears and backs off.

Cheepcheepcheepcheep. This constant noise better stop!

Ellie wants to know if the chick has a name.

"Who knows?" I say.

"I like Cheep," says Ellie, and the name is decided. We also agree that Cheep's a boy.

"Listen," I explain to Ellie, "I'm going to take Cheep out, so I can slide his tray in. You can pet him—and hold him for me. Okay?"

With a big smile, she cups both hands together.

Slowly, I lift the latch. I slip in my hand . . . *Ouch!*

The little puffball bounces out.

"Get him!" I yell, rubbing my finger. "Where did he go?"

All I need—a lost chicken! Brownish-gray blends with everything. A baby chick could find hundreds of hiding places in our living room: the sofa, bookshelves, board-game boxes, plants, even Norman's sneakers have plenty of room for that puffball. (Together, Norman's shoes are as big as the cage!) I whirl around, clenching my hand, hoping the pain in my finger will stop.

What will I tell Carol? How can I say I lost the chick? Drew and his kindergarten class will be heartbroken.

I press my hurt finger to my mouth. The chick could be anywhere in the house by now.

"Here!" Ellie shouts. She swoops down—the chicken is trapped!

Where? Oh no. The typewriter. A tiny brown head with beady eyes pokes out from the hollow space between the roller and the keys.

"Get out of there!" I shout.

I'm all set to yank, when Ellie scoots between us. She lifts Cheep out, smoothing his feathers with her chubby fingers. He doesn't even peep. "Cluck, cluck." She cuddles him.

"Yuck, yuck." First I get to pick feathers off the typewriter keys. (It'd better still work! I have lots to write about once that silly chicken settles down.) Then the card table needs to be scrubbed. Ugh. I hold my nose the whole time.

Finally, I fit the newspaper-covered tray back in the cage, adding dishes of fresh food and water. "All set, Cheep." I signal. "In you go.

"And in you stay," I mutter. The cage latches with a loud snap. Whew. Thank goodness *that's* over.

* * *

Just before suppertime, Mom calls me to set the table. Next to a large pot of spaghetti noodles, I see a newspaper clipping. Part one of a series.

"I must be losing my mind," Mom says. "Part two has to be *somewhere*. I had it in my hand an hour ago. Where was I?"

I bite a fingernail. "At the magazine rack?"

"Yes!" Mom springs up. "I was reading that piece when the phone rang."

"Uh, Mom?" I follow her to the living room. Ellie sits by the cage, cooing.

"Well, it's not here." Mom flips through the magazines.

"I know. Mom, I goofed." I point to the cage. "Your newspaper's right there."

Cheep must have taken a bath in his water dish. The newsprint is soaked. Sloshing through the puddles, the chick stops here and there to stab a few seeds.

Mom groans. She needs that piece of newspaper for the feature she's writing. "There's no time to get another copy. We'd better get it out of there."

Ellie holds Cheep, while Mom fishes out the newspaper. "What a mess," she complains. "I'll have to dry it somehow."

She dashes upstairs to find her hair dryer. I'm stuck cleaning the cage—again.

During supper, Cheep screeches. "Oh, stop it!" I shout.

"What's wrong with that guy?" Norman asks.

"Everything." I roll my eyes. "I wish Carol could take him back."

"Why doesn't she?" Norman asks between slurps of spaghetti.

"Carol's father's allergic."

"I'll bet," Norman snorts. "Like I'm allergic to homework. Or you!"

"He sneezed. Because of the feathers. Carol said so, and I heard a sneeze."

Cheep screeches again. Ellie jumps out of her booster chair, tipping over her bowl of spaghetti. She heads for the living room.

"Achoo, achoo!" Norman doubles over. "I'm having an attack! I got a feather in my nose!"

"I believe her," I shout. Then I frown. Carol also had told me the chick was "cute and fluffy"—and he's neither of those.

"Lizard," says Norman, "you've been had."

Mom walks in. "Did somebody sneeze? I hope no one's catching a cold." When no one answers, she shows me the blow-dried newspaper article. The paper crackles, but at least she can read it.

Then Mom sees spaghetti dripping from Ellie's place. "What happened here?"

"Mommy! Liddie!" Ellie shouts from the living room.

(Liddie? Yuck. How come she can say Cheep's name and not mine?) "Cheep's sick."

Norman runs to the scene. "She's right!" he reports. "It barfed!"

It's nighttime now, and I'm on duty. Nurse duty, though the chicken seems normal again. Cheep-cheep-cheeping away, after Mom and I cleaned up after it. For the *third* time, but who's counting? And I think Cheep's an *it* after all.

I've switched places with Winston. He's sleeping upstairs with Ellie, while I'm setting up my sleeping bag in the living room, next to the cage.

"Can Carol come over?" I ask.

Mom thinks I'm nuts. It's a school night. It's late. She pats Cheep's cage. "We have a full house right now, don't you think?"

"Guess so." I crawl into the sleeping bag and let Mom zip it up. As soon as Mom leaves the room, the chicken shakes its feathers—flexes its wings. *Chip-chip-chipchipchip*. It sounds like a motor, revving up.

It scurries across the cage. Wings flap. Hop. Hop. Then a plop. Another water landing.

I'm up again, to throw that dish towel over the cage. "Good night." I stare at the clock. Only nine more hours to go.

Maybe I'll call Carol anyway. Maybe I'll say, "Too bad

your dad's allergic to chickens. We're having a blast here. Sorry you're missing the whole thing."

She's my best friend. Think she'll believe me?

My finger hurts like crazy when I type. Thanks a heap, Cheep!

OUR SECRET CODE
* * *

MAY

For us to know, for you to ~~find out~~.

"Best friends should be able to speak freely," Carol says. "We shouldn't have to worry about snoops."

We're standing at the corner where the school bus drops us off. "We could whisper," I say, looking over my shoulder. The bus is gone, and the nearest kid is half a block away.

"Not in English." Carol sniffs. "Everybody speaks that. We need our own language, that nobody knows but us."

"Is somebody snooping on us?" I ask.

"Not *now*, maybe." Carol frowns. "But, Lizzie, when it happens, you'll wish we could have private conversations." Then she sighs. "Besides, wouldn't it be fun to have our own way to communicate?"

"Like a walkie-talkie?"

"Lizzie!" she shouts. "That's not at all what I mean. We need a code. A *secret* code."

"Okay, okay." I don't like to argue with Carol—and her idea of a code could be fun. But what should it be? The Morse code? Dots and dashes won't work in a conversation. Maybe we could invent a code—with special passwords. I wonder how spies and secret agents think them up.

Back home, I sit at the typewriter. *Clickclickclick . . .* I try playing with the letters of my name and Carol's. **EIZZIL**. **LORAC**. Backward works fine, if we want to write to each other and use mirrors. But out loud? No good.

An hour later Carol phones me. "I've got it! Listen to this, *Izzie-lay*."

"Is that my name?"

"Sure is. In *Pig Latin!*" she blurts out. "You've heard of it, haven't you?"

"'Course," I say. "So what's your name?" (I'm not sure I like *Izzie-lay*. It sounds too much like some icky name Norman might dream up for me.)

"Arol-cay."

At least hers sounds as bad as mine. "Well, maybe . . ." I'm still suspicious.

"Why maybe?" Carol argues. "It's the perfect code for us. I'll show you."

Here's how it works: Drop the first letter of any word and move it to the end. Follow that letter with the "ay" sound, to make a new syllable. If the first letter is a vowel, leave it alone and just add "ay" at the end.

"Say something in Pig Latin," Carol orders.

"*Omething-say.*" I laugh. "Or is it, *ome-say ing-thay?*"

The more we practice, the better I like it. Pig Latin makes the simplest words sound so goofy. *Ee-say y-may og-day? Ere-whay? At-ay e-thay ee-tray! Oing-day at-whay?* We giggle.

To translate from Pig Latin to English—forget about the "ay" and put the letter before it back at the front of the word. It's so easy, I worry it might be too easy. For a *secret* code, that is.

We can't speak it in class, of course. But we sneak in time on the bus—and at lunch. I point to the yellow glop on Carol's tray. "*Arf-bay.*"

"*Y-tray it-ay!*" Carol shoves a spoonful at me right there in the line.

Clack. The serving lady raps the metal glop container with a ladle. "Move along, girls," she snaps at us. To Carol, she says, "Turkey stew."

I nudge Carol. "Do you think she heard what I called it?"

"Don't worry." Carol shrugs. "You said it in Pig Latin."

"Maybe she understands Pig Latin." I glance back over

my shoulder. "She looks mad." *Clackclackclack*. I hear the ladle banging behind us.

When we reach our lunch table, Carol says, "We need to talk faster. We can't slow down in Pig Latin to make each word. If we speak fast, without breaks, people can't figure it out."

I sit down across from her and open my math book. After lunch, we have a test on decimals and fractions. (Carol hates decimals. I'm supposed to quiz her.)

Carol samples the glop. "Did she say this was turkey?"

"Urkey-tay arf-bay!" I say.

Carol stops eating. "Faster."

"Urkey-tay-arf-bay, urkey-tay-arf-bay!"

She bursts out laughing. "You can say that again." Some kids at the next table are watching us.

"What's the big joke?" a girl asks Carol.

"Lunch!" Carol winks at me. "Lizzie, can I have a bite of your sandwich?"

"Take point five," I say, offering her the uneaten half.

Carol comes over after school. She can't wait to tell me about something that happened in the nurse's office, where she got sent—clutching her stomach—after lunch.

"Did you really barf?" I want to know. She missed the math test but seems well again now.

"Urkey-tay arf-bay" is all she'll say. We're supposed to be testing our code this afternoon: We'll speak only Pig Latin when anyone else is around. And here come Winston and Ellie.

"Ome-cay ere-hay," I say. Winston snuggles against me, sticking his nose in my lap. Ellie flops on the floor at my feet.

"They know," I tell Carol.

"Know what?"

"The code. Winston came over and—"

"Lizzie, don't be ridiculous." Carol snorts. "Dogs don't know Pig Latin!"

But what about Ellie? When we say, *"Et-pay e-thay oggie-day,"* she does!

"O-gay ay-play," I say next.

"Ogay ayplay," says Ellie.

Carol frowns. "She speaks as fast as we do."

"She's copying me," I grumble. "She doesn't really get it." But when Ellie trots off to play with her beanbag monkey, I groan.

In comes Norman, wearing a smudged Brewers T-shirt with a rip on the sleeve. (Dad got him a new shirt at the Opening Day game, but Norman likes his messy old one better.) *"At-whay a-ay ob-slay,"* we say to each other and giggle.

"What's so funny?" Norman tosses his backpack, which lands with a thud by my feet.

"Othing-nay." We giggle some more.

Norman stands over us, arms crossed. "Say that again."

"Ay-say at-whay?" I nudge Carol. *"At-thay?"*

Carol nudges me back. *"E-hay oesn't-day et-gay it-ay."*

Frowning, Norman plops on a chair across the room from us.

"Morons, both of you," he mutters, and grabs the sports page to read.

Since Norman doesn't seem to be listening to us, I ask Carol (in Pig Latin) what happened in the nurse's office.

"Ice-lay eck-chay!" She grins. *"Omorrow-tay."* We hear Norman's newspaper rustle.

In rapid, flawless Pig Latin, Carol explains the nurse's plan. Tomorrow, every fourth-grader will be inspected for lice, because the nurse suspects a "problem" in our class. While taking a rest for her stomachache, Carol watched a boy and a girl get their hair checked. The nurse found nits on both and sent them home.

"Uck-yay!" I pull my braids off my shoulders. The idea of those tiny bugs in your scalp is too disgusting for words! My head itches just from thinking about it.

I glance at Norman, who doesn't look up from the sports page. Speaking faster than ever, I thank Carol for the *"eads-hay up-ay,"* and we laugh.

The next morning at the bus stop, Carol shouts "Yikes!" at my back.

"What's the matter?"

Carol cups her hand over her mouth. "Your jacket. Take a look."

Hurriedly, I slip out of my windbreaker. Pinned to the back is this message:

Lizzie Has Lice

Above the words is an arrow, pointing up. At my head, I suppose.

I rip the sign off. "How could he?"

"Your brother's really a louse," Carol says. "Lucky I saw this before we got to school!" She peers at the sign. "Boy, he has horrible handwriting."

While that's true, it's not his worst quality. *Louse,* though, comes close. *Norman the Nit.* I wish I could put *that* on a sign!

I squash the Lizzie sign into a ball. "What a snoop," I say, "and a sneak. Pretending he didn't know what we were talking about when he got every word!" I toss the ball into a trash can. "Carol, how come so many people know Pig Latin?"

"Who else?" Carol fidgets with her backpack.

"Ellie, Winston—"

"You can't count your dog!" Carol insists. "And Ellie was . . . a coincidence!"

"Even the cafeteria lady," I add, "knew exactly what *arf-bay* meant. I bet the nurse would recognize *ice-lay*, too."

The bus pulls up. As we board, I tell Carol I'm through with Pig Latin. "For a secret code, it's a dud!" I sink into a seat in our usual row. "What else you got?"

Sitting beside me, she scratches her head. "Uh-oh, Carol." I can't help grinning. "You'd better not!"

The nit had a fit and turned into a zit.
Need me to decode it?

MOM'S BAD DAY
* * *

JUNE

Can today be saved?

It's the last day of the month *and* my half-birthday. So far, I call it a bummer.

"Ick!" Mom burns my toast at breakfast. "Sorry about that, Lizzie." I feed the toast to Winston, who growls.

"Ouch!" Mom's finger is caught in the door of the dishwasher. "That's what I get for rushing." She shows me the broken nail, turning purply-blue underneath.

"I'm sick of toast," Norman whines. "Can't we have cereal?"

"Something special," I say. "For my half-birthday."

Nobody is listening. Mom opens a box of Wheaties. It rustles.

"Mice!" Mom screams and slams the box on the counter.

Norman jumps up. "Let me see." He peers inside. "Wow, a whole family! A mommy mouse and four babies."

Ellie smiles. "Mouse babies."

"Ugh. Don't remind me." Mom reaches under the counter for a garbage bag.

You-know-who shoves the box straight at me. "Hey, Lizzie. Want some Wheaties? Plain . . . or with mice?"

Mice on my half-birthday? Not what I wished for, but I want to peek inside the box. The baby ones might make good pets. (Couldn't be worse than a baby chick, I bet.)

Mom plops the box in the trash. "Take it out," she tells Norman.

Above her, on the kitchen counter, the coffeepot hisses and splashes muddy water all over everything—including Mom. She has big brown spots on her new red blouse. She runs upstairs to change her clothes. She trips.

"Norman, why is your baseball glove out here in the hallway?" Mom yells. "Why is everything going wrong today?"

Since it's summer, our cousin Lucy watches Ellie and me while Mom is at work. (Thanks goodness Norman goes off to day camp, or we might have had him as babysitter.) This morning Lucy comes late—and she doesn't remember it's my half-birthday, either. Mom rushes out, though she doesn't look ready to leave. A scarf hangs untied around her neck, and her hair looks stringy because she didn't finish drying it. She blows me a kiss, but she forgets to smile. There must be something I can do to make Mom feel better when she comes home.

"Let's make the beds," I say. Ellie helps me (or tries to). She munches her breakfast while we work.

"Oops," says Ellie. Mom's pillow is covered with toast crumbs. Her blanket is smudged with peanut butter and chunks of banana. Ellie only eats this stuff because I do! I pile all the bedding into the laundry basket. One more thing gone wrong.

I pick daisies from our yard and string a necklace for Mom. But Winston finds it first. "Bad dog!" I scold. He goes right on chewing. All he leaves are the stems.

Lucy lets me make cupcakes. Besides cheering Mom up, they'll be my half-birthday treat. I pull out four cookbooks to study the different recipes before choosing vanilla cake with butterscotch frosting. "Can't go wrong with vanilla," Mom says when she makes it for each one of our birthdays.

I put the eggs we need on the counter. Of course, three eggs roll off and drop to the floor. *Clickclack Crack!*

"Stay back!" I warn Winston. Too late. Winston dashes off leaving a trail of eggy paw prints. After that, we don't have enough eggs for the batter, but we bake the cupcakes anyway. We sample some. They taste like sponges.

Winston curls up next to me in the window seat. My tears drip onto his fur. I type for a while, but it doesn't make me feel better. Soon Mom will come home from work. The day is even worse than it was when she left.

Norman comes home first. He drops his baseball glove on the kitchen floor. The glove lands in a puddle of egg. But Norman doesn't notice. He grabs a cupcake for a snack.

"These are disgusting!" he yells.

He bends down to pick up his glove. It drips.

"What is this junk on my glove?" Norman shakes the glove at me. "It'd better wash off. Or else, whoever did this to my glove is buying me a new one!"

"It was Winston," I mumble. "And it was an accident."

Norman doesn't hear me. He jumps up and bangs on the back door. "Winston, get out of there!"

I rush outside, after Norman. "What's Winston doing with the Wheaties box?" I ask.

"He, uh, must have smelled a mouse." Norman kicks the ground. "I tried to hide them."

"But Mom told you to get rid of them."

"She *said* to take them outside, and I did. Those little guys." Norman sounds sad. "I hope they're okay."

"Maybe they are. Maybe they just ran away." I pick up the empty box. "Winston wouldn't hurt them, would he?"

"Hope not." Norman whistles to Winston. "Lizzie, don't tell Mom. Just in case, uh, the mice ran *inside*."

Norman—and Winston—check out the kitchen. I sit on the front steps to wait for Mom. Her car rattles and screeches to a stop in our driveway.

"Hear that?" says Mom. *Clickclack Clunk.* "Even the car sounds sick today."

Mom slams the car door. As she walks toward me, her face is sweaty. She spits out a piece of gum, sticking it on the corner of the newspaper. "Ugh. I've been chewing the same piece for hours."

Then she tells me how she had to fill in for an editor on vacation. "So many stories showed up in bad shape," she sighs. "I fixed up most of them, sharpening first sentences, cutting out boring parts and endings that trail off into nowhere. And then when I'm on deadline, your father calls. Says it can't wait—he needs to make plans for your summer visit. This minute."

"He's in Minnesota," I say. "He doesn't know your deadlines."

"I suppose not." Mom wipes her brow. "I shouldn't have let it bother me. But there I was, working my head off . . ."

I turn away. Mom bends down. From her sweaty hug, I can feel how tired she is. "What's wrong, Lizzie? Did you have a bad day, too?"

"I wanted to do something special for you. But everything went wrong. Your bed has mashed banana in it, and Winston ate all the daisies out of a necklace that was supposed to be for you.

"Then we made cupcakes." I start to cry. "They taste terrible. Even Norman couldn't finish one."

Mom holds me close. "Is that all?"

I cry even harder. "Norman's baseball glove has egg on it. That's my fault, too. The eggs were supposed to go into the cupcakes. But after they broke all over the floor Winston got into them and left a big mess and then Norman said whoever made the mess—"

"Oh, Lizzie," Mom says.

"I only wanted—" I gulp. "I only wanted to turn this bad day into a good day. It's my half-birthday, you know."

"Is it?" Mom takes my hand. "You could try again tomorrow, since June only has thirty days. With a birthday on the last day of December, you can celebrate your half-birthday on the first day of July."

"It can't be worse than today," I say.

Mom says, "You know, Lizzie, today turned out fine. You spent it trying to do nice things for me. That's what

I'll remember." She steps back, smiling. "That, and mashed banana in my bed! How much banana, by the way?"

"It's not in your bed anymore." I try to smile back. "But wait 'til you see the laundry."

Ellie runs out to us. "Mommy see the laundry."

"I can't wait," Mom says. And she doesn't wait long. Lucy appears with a soggy blue lump.

"I'm sorry," Lucy says anxiously. "I was folding the rest of the bedding when Ellie took off—with this. I'd put it aside, to go to the cleaners, but Ellie decided to wash it herself."

It's Mom's blanket, sopping wet! "Looks like it's been in the bathtub," I say.

Lucy groans. "How did you guess?"

"Well," says Mom, "I'll bet it's clean." She pats Ellie's hair. "Thanks for trying to help."

"She wasn't helping," I mutter. "I was helping. She was copying."

Mom smiles and pulls me closer. "I think that counts as trying, and today we need all the help we can get. Now, let's see those cupcakes. Maybe together we can fix them."

We make bread pudding for dessert. I borrow eggs from our neighbor. Ellie crumbles the cupcakes into a big bowl. She "helps" me stir in the milk and raisins. (*Scritch.* I hear a funny noise coming from the cupboard, but I don't tell anybody.) We watch the clock while the custard cooks. Mom cuts us big slices, steaming hot from the oven.

"Uh-oh," I say after one bite. The spongy taste is still there.

Mom laughs. "What a day. Who wants ice cream?"

Rats! We're out of peppermint.

THE BIG PEST CONTEST
* * *

JULY

I nominate Norman.

You-know-who has done it again.

The mice are back. This time, we find three grayish lumps (with tails) in a bag of potato chips. One look is enough for me. I *don't* want them as pets (though I wonder what happened to the other two).

When Mom grabs the phone to call the pest control company, Norman says, "Don't bother. I'll take care of it."

"Like last time." I smirk. "You did such a good job."

"What's *that* supposed to mean?" Mom jumps on Norman, who swears the cereal-box mice were thrown out of the house.

But when Mom leaves the room, Norman creeps up behind me. "Eek, eek," he says. "Watch out, Lizard."

"What's *that* supposed to mean?"

"You might want to look around for those little guys. Like under your pillow."

"Yikes!" cries Carol when I tell her the mice-under-the-pillow part. We're at the park, climbing our favorite tree. I'm perched on a branch below hers. "Did you check?" she gasps.

"No." I reach up to stop her from swinging her feet in my face.

"You'd better," Carol insists. "If my brother said something like that, it would happen." Carol's brother is five. "Monkey say, monkey do." She giggles.

I almost say Norman won't do it—he's just being a pest. But he's been so annoying, so many times. "I'm FED UP"—I point to the sky—"to here!"

"Then do something about it," Carol says. "Get even."

"How?"

"Play a trick on him."

I look up at her. "What kind of trick?"

"A clever trick. An awesome trick."

"Yeah, yeah," I say. "Like what?"

Carol shuts her eyes, makes a fist, and puts her chin on it. She does the same thing in school when she can't think of an answer.

Suddenly, it comes to her, and she slaps the branch. *Clack.* "Who does Norman like?"

"You mean a girlfriend? He doesn't have one."

"So," says Carol, "make one up. Pretend there's a girl in his class who likes him. Somebody cool. Call him up—"

"He'll recognize me."

"We-ell," she says, "I could call him."

This has possibilities. "Would you?"

"What are best friends for?" Carol slides down to my branch. "Let's see. I could say I'm Gloria. I've *always* wanted to be Gloria."

"She's too cool for Norman," I say. They're in the same grade, but that's the only thing they have in common. Gloria wins dance contests and gets the lead role in school plays. Because Gloria is Carol's next-door neighbor, we see her going to rehearsals and parties. Sometimes she waves to Carol and me, but I'm sure she's never noticed Norman.

"That's the point," Carol says. "That's why he'll fall for it. If she were some nerd, he'd hang right up!"

We decide that "Gloria" will call Norman and invite him to a party.

"Make it a costume party," I say. "Then Norman can show up at her house in something stupid."

"We can hide out at my house and watch him ringing

her doorbell," Carol adds. "Won't he look ridiculous, showing up in a costume? Gloria won't know what he's doing there!"

From our branch I spot Norman and Chip swinging baseball bats as they head for the diamond at one end of the park. "Let's get out of here," I whisper. "Don't let them see us!" We scramble down the tree and run all the way to Carol's house. It's the safest place we can think of to rehearse our phone call.

Carol tries out a breathy voice. "Norman, I'm having a party tomorrow night. A costume party, at my house. Can you come?" She munches a graham cracker. "My voice isn't as low as Gloria's," she says between bites.

I shrug. "Norman won't know that. She hasn't been calling *him* up."

"What do you think he'll wear?"

"His baseball uniform, probably. He wears it every Halloween. He'll jazz it up with some silly cap and his glove."

"Dull, dull, dull." Carol sniffs. "Maybe 'Gloria' should tell him that for her party, a baseball costume won't do."

"Tell him everybody else is coming as monsters. Or Martians!"

"Say, Norman," Carol lowers her voice, "couldn't you come as a hippopotamus?" She laughs so hard, she has to wipe her eyes.

I laugh, too, but I feel a little bit sorry for Norman.

He'll make such a fool of himself in front of Gloria. Showing up uninvited, in some crazy costume. Maybe we shouldn't go through with it.

Suddenly, a hand sneaks into the graham-cracker box. A five-year-old hand. I tap Carol's shoulder, but Drew whizzes past us—like Winston chasing a squirrel.

"Hey, you piggy," Carol shouts after him. "Give those back!"

"You can't make me!" Drew yells with his mouth full.

"What a pest," Carol grumbles to me. "You don't know what you're missing by not having a little brother."

"I have Ellie."

"Girls are different," Carol says.

Really? She still has it easy, compared to me. She's not stuck in the middle of *her* family. Drew may be a pain, but he's in the minor leagues, compared to Norman. So I say, "I'll bet you my *big* brother is a much bigger pest than your *little* brother."

"You're on!" cries Carol. "And you'll lose. Your brother is bigger because he's older. But that doesn't make him a bigger pest!"

We go back to rehearsing. Carol practices her Gloria lines while I play Norman. I pretend to knock on Gloria's door. "Oooo," shrieks Carol-as-Gloria. "Who in the world are you?"

That little-bit-sorry feeling comes back. Then I remember the mice that he threatened to put in my bed. And his LIZZIE HAS LICE sign—how he tried to embarrass me in front of the whole school! So what if we embarrass him in front of Gloria? The big pest deserves it!

"Are we set?" Carol asks. "A call from Gloria at seven o'clock sharp?"

"All set," I say as I leave for home. I was only a little bit sorry, anyway.

Supper is hamburgers and corn on the cob. They're my favorites, but I'm way too excited to eat. Nobody's watching me. Mom's on the floor, looking for Ellie's corncob. Norman is helping himself to seconds or thirds. From under the table Winston sniffs me. I break my hamburger into pieces and place them in my lap.

"Anything wrong with your burger, Lizzie?" Mom asks.

I say no and try a sip of milk.

"You eat like a mouse," says Norman.

"Mom—" As I open my mouth, the milk dribbles out.

"Lizzie, you're such a slob!" Norman shouts. Then he cups his hand and whispers, "Eek, eek."

"Mom, he's upsetting my stomach. Can I be excused?"

At 6:30 the phone rings. I rush back to the kitchen, but this call is for Mom. From Uncle Steve—I can tell by the way he makes Mom laugh.

"Gracious," she says. "Compared to your office, *The*

Milwaukee Journal's a breeze. We only work sixty hours a week!"

"Hurry up," I grumble. "Pretend you're on a deadline."

"Well, Steve," says Mom, suddenly serious. "That's a longer conversation."

What? Mom will spoil everything if she talks any longer. It's 6:52. Carol's probably right by her phone, rehearsing her Gloria imitation one more time.

I *can't* let her get a busy signal.

I walk over and tap Mom's shoulder. "Almost through?" She nods.

"I need to ask you something."

"Good," Mom says into the telephone.

I mouth the word "Bye."

Mom hangs up. *Click.* "Lizzie, what's up? Is your stomach better?"

My stomach? How does *Mom* know it's full of butterflies? I watch the clock and can't think of a thing to say to her.

"Lizzie," says Mom, "you're acting peculiar."

At seven o'clock on the dot the telephone rings.

"I'll get it!" I lunge. "Just a moment, please," I say before racing upstairs to find Norman. "Telephone for you."

I slip back downstairs to the kitchen, to listen in.

"Hullo," I hear Norman say.

"This is Gloria." Carol's voice is so low, I'm afraid I'll giggle.

"Gloria?" Norman sounds surprised. "From school?"

I cup my hand over my mouth.

"Yes, but it's not about school, why I'm calling."

"Great," Norman chimes in. "Fine, I mean . . ."

For once, Norman is tongue-tied. The same Norman who called me a slob and made mouse noises at supper, bumbling along. Serves him right.

I hold the phone close as Carol continues, "I'm having a party and want to—"

"Hi," says another voice. Another *squeaky* little voice. "Mommy wants you."

Carol tries to recover. "We have a bad connection."

"Gloria? Are you there?" Norman asks.

"Who's Gloria?" asks the squeaky voice.

"We have a party line," Carol says in a high voice, too. "We have this problem a lot. Our calls get all mixed up." Her voice drops. "Get off the phone, will you please."

"Nope. You can't make me. Mommy wants you to take a bath."

Carol says, "I'll have to call you back, Norman."

Hang up! I want to scream. But the squeaky voice speaks first. Just one word. The worst possible word.

"Carol—"

"You morons!" Norman yells. "You didn't fool me for a minute." He slams down the phone. *Clack!*

"Uh-oh," I whisper to Carol. "We blew it."

"Did we ever. I feel like such an idiot. Drew is the biggest pest in the whole wide world!"

Then she laughs. "I told you so, didn't I?"

I call it a tie.

COPY CAT
* * *

Go away, get lost. You're not my twin!

Ellie likes to do everything that I do. I wish she didn't.

If I chase Winston around the yard, so does Ellie.

If I choose a purple lollipop or a green balloon, so does she.

If I sing, Ellie sings "The Alphabet Song"—the only song she knows. It's really annoying to hear.

Mom says, "She admires you. It's a compliment. You should feel flattered."

I don't.

For the first part of this month, I was in Minnesota visiting Dad—alone. Norman will go after he comes back from sleep-away camp, and Ellie was staying home with Mom (and Winston). Each day at Dad's we tried something new: fishing, sailing, Rollerblading. (Dad's first time on skates, so he fell a lot!) Dad was worried I'd get lonely. "You're an only child for a change," he said. "Seems strange, doesn't it?"

"Yeah," I said, though I don't think we meant the same thing by *strange*. It felt *terrific* to go to a baseball game with Dad without Norman. (I may even become a Twins fan instead!) And everything we did was much more fun without Ellie along.

Now I'm back home. Norman's still gone, but Ellie gets in my way more than ever.

I plan a tea party for Mom and me and my favorite doll, Anna. It's supposed to be dress up. Anna wears her pink party dress with a white ruffled apron—the one with the puffy red heart sewn onto it. I'm wearing my hair up, instead of in braids. Just when it's time to serve treats, Ellie drags in her baby doll, Lulu (wearing a diaper). The bean-bag monkey shows up at Mom's place, while a rabbit puppet crowds in next to Anna. Ellie tugs on the table-cloth—and splashes us all with lemonade tea!

"This was *my* party," I complain to Mom. "Who asked Ellie?"

Mom laughs, though I don't see what's so funny. "Lizzie, you used to follow Norman around when you were Ellie's age."

"I did not! Why would I want to?"

"You liked to do what the big kids did. You liked his company." Mom nudges me. "You two were chummy."

I hold my nose. Norman and I haven't been "chummy" recently. I apologized for "Gloria," but boy, was he mad. I figured he'd come up with some trick of his own in return. But he hasn't (yet). I think he mostly blames Carol for the phone call, though. He never mentions her without saying "that dork."

"Oh, I bet you miss him," Mom says. "When my brother went to summer camp . . ."

I stop listening. Uncle Steve wasn't like Norman . . . or was he?

"Sorry about the spill," Mom goes on. "Ellie doesn't mean to be clumsy—or bother you. Be patient, Lizzie. Soon she'll be three years old, and more of a pal."

But that only makes me feel worse! Who wants to pal around with a three-year-old? And while she has a birthday in the fall to look forward to, mine is still more than four months away. No fair!

In the afternoon mail two big boxes arrive. Each has glittery wrapping paper and a big silver bow.

Mom reads the card aloud: "Love from Aunt Molly."

I peel off the wrapping paper and save the bow. Inside my box, under layers of tissue paper, is a red-and-white checked dress. I lift out the dress carefully, while Ellie rips through the tissue paper in her box. Her dress, in a smaller size, is exactly the same as mine. The ruffles, the pockets, even the buttons are in exactly the same places.

"Sister dresses," says Mom. "Just like Aunt Molly and I wore when we were little girls."

Ellie swings her dress over her head. "Sister dresses, sister dresses," she chants. "Just like Aunt Mommy!"

I cover my ears and say nothing.

"Do you like your new dress?" Mom asks. "Isn't red your favorite color?"

Not anymore, I almost say. Not if Ellie's going to wear it, too.

I pretend to like the dress, though. I nod when Mom says, "Isn't it nice of Aunt Molly to send you a back-to-school present?" I agree to write my own thank-you note and to wear the dress when Aunt Molly comes for a visit.

Ellie can't wait to wear her new dress. Mom helps her put it on right away.

I drag the box with my dress in it upstairs to our room. I stuff the box under my bed. Ellie follows me. "Go away," I say. She won't, of course, because it's her room, too. I kick her beanbag monkey across the floor.

I fold a sheet of the wrapping paper and cut paper dolls. Ellie reaches for my scissors.

"No!" I push her away. "You're too little to use scissors."

Ellie plays with the ruffle on her dress. Then she reaches for the scissors again.

I grip them so tightly that my hand cramps. Watching her playing with the ruffle, I wonder. How would her dress look without it? Cut it off, and the dress wouldn't look like mine anymore.

I point the scissors at the ruffle. "Do you want this . . . to go away?"

"Bye-bye." Ellie giggles.

"Okay. Here we go. Bye-bye, ruffle." I start to snip. "Hold still." Instantly, Ellie jumps and tries to tug the scissors away from me. Before I let go, they pierce a hole in the front of the skirt.

"Uh-oh." How did that happen? When I touch the skirt, the hole gets even bigger.

Ellie sticks her finger through it. "Look!" She smiles. "I show Mommy!"

I pick up the scissors, snap the blades open and shut a few times. *Click Clip.* Maybe Ellie doesn't think anything's wrong with her dress. But I know Mom will.

"Here, Ellie," I say. "Let me see it better." Somehow, I talk Ellie into changing her clothes. (She puts on Winnie-the-Pooh pajamas.) Then she hears Winston and runs out of the room, singing "The Alphabet Song." I throw Ellie's dress in our closet.

Moments later, Mom walks in without knocking. "You

can't go outside in pajamas," she calls over her shoulder to Ellie. "Now, what shall we wear?"

"My dress," Ellie shouts. "I want my new dress."

I'm trapped. I stare at the window. No good—we're too high up to jump to the ground. And the nearest tree is halfway across our yard.

Of course Mom will look in the closet, but I slip inside it anyway. I hide the dress under a pile of board games.

"Lizzie," Mom says. "What are you doing?"

"Looking for . . . my sandals." As I start to bend down, I see the sash of Ellie's dress—poking out between Clue and Monopoly.

"There they are." Mom points to my shoes, then glances at the clothes racks. "Lizzie, where are the new dresses?"

I stall, fiddling with the strap of my sandal. What can I say? Any minute Mom will see the sash sticking out. "You know, the *sister* dresses. From Aunt Molly." Mom sweeps by the shelf that holds our sweaters. Warm, warmer . . . the board games are next.

As Mom reaches that shelf, I scoot back toward the window. Mom touches the sash. "Why is this here?" she asks.

"Liddie did it," says Ellie.

Frowning, Mom pulls the dress from the closet. "That's no way to care for clothes, Lizzie."

"Liddie did it!" Ellie repeats—just as Mom sees the hole.

Mom spreads Ellie's dress on the floor in front of me. "Explain this."

I squirm. "It was Ellie's idea."

"What do you mean?" Mom crosses her arms.

I show Mom the scissors. "I was using these. Then she comes in and wants to cut—" I gulp.

"Cut what?" Mom snaps. "Are you telling me Ellie wanted to put a hole in her dress?"

"She wanted *me* to." I glance at Ellie. "Bye-bye, ruffle?" Ellie giggles again.

Mom isn't laughing *at all*. "What's the matter with you, Lizzie? A brand-new dress, and you ruined it. How could you?"

"I hate that dress!" I shriek. "I don't want to look just like Ellie!"

Mom sits on the floor with me. She says nothing for a moment—a *long* moment.

"Lizzie, look at me."

I start to cry. "I didn't mean to wreck it. I just wanted her dress to look different from mine."

"With a hole?" Mom gasps.

"I meant to cut off the ruffle."

"Honestly." Mom shakes her head. "The dresses are alike, not you and Ellie."

I sniff, but the tears keep coming. "I don't want to look

like Ellie! I don't want to *be* like her. I can't stand her copying me!"

"Lizzie, be reasonable," Mom says. "This is a phase. When Ellie is older—"

"She'll be worse!" I shout. "She'll copy me *more!*"

Ellie crawls into Mom's lap. "Pretty." She points to her dress. "Liddie fixed it."

Mom shakes her head and carries Ellie out over her shoulder. "Lizzie *will* fix it," she says.

But how?

I touch the hole—I can wiggle two fingers through it. There must be some way to cover it up.

I reach for Anna and slip off her apron. I put the dress and the white ruffled apron together. A nice combination, but the apron won't fit Ellie. I can't see a way to lengthen it, either. Too bad, since Ellie would love that puffy red heart.

Then I remember *my* dress from Aunt Molly. I pull out the box from under my bed. I hold Ellie's dress beside mine—why can't we shorten my dress to fit Ellie? If Mom teaches me how, I'll do all the sewing myself.

I run downstairs to show Mom the dresses. I ask her to teach me hemming. It seems like the right answer to me. Ellie gets a new dress, and we won't have to wear the same thing.

Mom squeezes my hand. "Maybe, Lizzie. Let me think about it. You can certainly help with the sewing if we decide to alter your dress. But Aunt Molly sent two dresses. What will she think when she comes for a visit and sees we only have one?" She looks me in the eye. "Meanwhile, where's your thank-you note?"

CLACKCLACKCLACKCLACK CLICKCLICK. I bang the typewriter keys so hard that all my fingers hurt.

> Dear Aunt Molly,
>
> Thank you for our new red dresses. Red is my favorite color--and Ellie's, because she ~~copies me in everything. When you and Mom were kids, did you copy her all the time? Did she mind? Did you stop copying her after you were three? Just curious.~~ likes the same things I do. ~~Mom says it's flattering but I think it's really annoying.~~ Ellie wore her dress today, while I am saving mine for a special occasion.
>
> Love,
>
> Lizzie

There. I feel better, even though I still have to fix Ellie's dress—and copy over this letter. (Where are copy cats when you need them?) I think I'll use glitter ink for a change. And sign my name with a big red heart . . .

"That's it!" I jump up from the typewriter and grab my scissors. I race to find Anna. I can patch the hole in the dress with the heart from the apron. According to my ruler, the heart's the right size—as long as the hole doesn't get any bigger.

"Call it a transplant!" Mom says when she approves my idea. And it works (except for the hole I have to make in Anna's apron). Ellie loves her new dress with the heart. And it's not exactly like mine anymore.

But nobody, not even Aunt Molly, can make me wear my dress on the same day Ellie wears hers.

WHAT'S WRONG
WITH MR. CALHOUN?
* * *

SEPTEMBER

He isn't like other teachers.

"Why did we have to get *him?*" Carol wails as we wait for the bus to take us to school.

She means Mr. Calhoun, our fifth-grade teacher. I've heard a little about him, from Norman. But Carol seems to know more, and she's full of complaints.

"He's strict—*everybody* says so. His hair is white already. He sounds like he's from England or Australia. Before he moved here, he taught in a prep school somewhere. He doesn't tell jokes, or smile . . ."

I'd looked forward to school starting, but now I'm not sure. Mr. Calhoun is the first male teacher I've had. "He taught Norman," I say, "and Norman liked him, I think."

Carol rolls her eyes. "Everybody *else* thinks he's weird," she says as the bus rumbles toward us.

"Young ladies and gentlemen," says Mr. Calhoun, "think of this year together as an adventure. Push yourself. Set new goals and standards . . ."

Carol's right about some things. His hair is white—and he wears wire-rimmed glasses, but otherwise he doesn't look old.

He may have an accent, though I can't tell where it's from. He uses big words and talks as if he's in the auditorium, making a speech.

". . . You cannot coast in my class. Effort will be rewarded, but sloth will not be tolerated. Proper work habits and attitude will be emphasized. My expectations are higher than you may be used to . . ."

From the desk next to mine, Carol leans over and whispers, "*Tons* of homework, that means."

Mr. Calhoun's head snaps toward our row. "Private conversations will not be allowed. And no one will talk out of turn. If you have something to say to the entire class, please raise your hand." (Carol sticks her hands in her lap.)

Mr. Calhoun calls the roll. "Elizabeth Anderson."

"Here." I want to tell him everybody calls me Lizzie

(except for my swimming teacher and Ellie, who tries to, I guess). But my voice feels scratchy—he must be making me nervous. When he asks if I'm related to Norman, I nod. (Carol mouths, "Duh.")

"Please give him my greetings." Mr. Calhoun takes off his glasses and rubs the marks on his nose. "I remember Norman quite well."

At lunch Carol and I sit together. "I don't talk out of turn," she grumbles. "He has it in for me."

"He doesn't know you," I say, opening my lunch box. "It's just the first day."

"It's going to be a long year," Carol says.

I pull the crusts off my sandwich. "I wonder what Mr. Calhoun remembers about Norman."

Carol stirs meat loaf into her mashed potatoes. (She always buys the school lunch.) "If he knows the same Norman *we* know, you're in trouble!"

"I don't know what Norman's like in school," I say. "He might be the type to talk out of turn."

Carol kicks me under the table. "I didn't talk. I *whispered*. He couldn't have heard me, could he? About homework?" She growls at her plate of meat-loaf-mashed-potato-mush. "If he gives us math, I'll puke!"

The first day, our homework assignment is graphs. "Look at these problems," Carol fumes on the bus ride home. "They'll take me all night! And we must have a hundred vocabulary words to look up, before he tests us tomorrow."

"Twenty words," I correct her. "And the test is on Friday. Review is tomorrow." I glance at the vocabulary list. "Look, Carol, they're not so hard. You don't have to look up *preposterous,* do you?"

She smiles for the first time all day. "Can I say 'I did a preposterous amount of homework' when he makes me use it in a sentence?"

Back home, I spread out my homework on the kitchen table. On his way to the refrigerator Norman leans over my shoulder.

"You got that one wrong." He points to my first answer.

I turn and glare back at him. "Can't you read?" he goes on, stabbing the assignment sheet with his finger. " 'Rainfall by Country.' You're supposed to calculate the averages and put them in a bar graph, see? You drew a line graph."

"You're in my way." I sneak a look at the examples. Bar graphs. Phooey.

"Line graphs don't work for categories like countries. You're trying to compare—"

"Stop bothering me! I'm busy."

"I was only trying to help." He opens the refrigerator.

"I don't need your help." I cover the graph paper with

one hand, so he won't see me erasing the line. "By the way, my teacher sends his greetings to you."

"You got Calhoun?" Norman whistles. "Boy, oh boy!"

I lean on my elbows. "Is he really so strict? Everybody says—"

"Who's everybody? Your friend the dork?"

"She's not—"

"Hey," he interrupts. "So, Calhoun knows you're my sister, huh?"

"He said he remembered you. Quite well."

Norman grins and sticks his thumb in the air. He whistles again. I have no idea why.

Once I'm through with the math problems, I telephone Carol. I want to compare answers, but she hasn't finished yet.

"Guess what I heard," she says in a rush. "About Mr. Calhoun."

"Give me a hint."

"About why he's the way he is."

"I don't know how he is," I say. "We've only had him for one day."

"Lizzie," Carol snaps, "he's taught at our school for years. *Everybody* knows he's strange. You want to know why, or not?"

"Okay, tell me." I know she will anyway.

"His wife left him." Carol pauses. "Lizzie, are you still there?"

I fiddle with the cord of the telephone. "I don't see what that has to do with the way he is at school."

"He's unhappy. An awful thing happened and he's never gotten over it." She clicks her teeth. *Clickclick.*

I frown at the phone. "How do *you* know? He didn't act unhappy in class."

"Gloria told me all about it," Carol says huffily. "If you don't believe me, ask *her.*"

I won't do that—I hardly know Gloria. But I don't think that story about Mr. Calhoun is true. Some marriages aren't happy, and people split up. I know more about that than either Carol or Gloria, probably.

"Believe what you want to," Carol says. "Now excuse me, I have math to do." I hear her teeth clicking again as we hang up.

The next day Mr. Calhoun asks me to put my graph of average rainfalls on the blackboard. After praising my drawing (which he calls a "display"), he asks me to explain why the solution calls for a bar graph. He likes what I say about categories and comparisons.

"Nice work," he says. "I can see you have your brother's flair for mathematics."

My face feels hot. Why did he have to say *that*? Staring

down, I walk back to my desk. I hear laughs from the back of the room.

On the way to recess a boy shouts, "There's Lizzie, the math whiz."

I nudge Carol to walk faster.

"Math whizzie," another chimes in. I shut my eyes—I know who they are. Doug and Sam from the back row. "Lizziewhizzie, take a quizzie!"

Carol wheels around, bumping me. The boys roar as I trip. "Get lost, creeps!" Carol yells, then pulls me up. Rubbing my knee, I walk stiffly toward the playground. I hear *Lizziewhizzie* echoing behind us.

"I wish he hadn't said that about me," I mutter once we're outside.

"They're bozos," says Carol, sounding a little like Norman.

"I meant Mr. Calhoun," I explain. "I didn't like what he said to me at the blackboard. That flair for mathematics stuff started it."

"Well," Carol says, "didn't I tell you he was strange?"

During the vocabulary lesson, Mr. Calhoun calls on Carol. Normally, she knows the answers and raises her hand. But this time her hand was down. She's doodling on her vocabulary list.

"Please tell us the meaning of *trite*. Carol?"

She stalls. "*Trite,*" he repeats.

Leaning forward, Carol puts her chin on her fist. "Does it mean . . . sorry?"

"I'm afraid not. That's *contrite,* a perfectly good word, but not *trite.*" His mouth curves, more like a smirk than a smile. Carol slumps back in her chair.

"Doug? Do you know the meaning of *trite?*" For some reason, Mr. Calhoun doesn't call on the kids who've raised their hands.

"Nope," says Doug.

Sam punches Doug's shoulder. "Way to go."

Though Sam talked out of turn, Mr. Calhoun ignores him. He calls on me next.

I glance at Carol. While I hate to embarrass her, I know the answer and can't see pretending I don't. "Overused," I say. "Like an expression that's become common. Or stale."

"Precisely," says Mr. Calhoun. "A way with words runs in the family, too."

My face is burning. (I don't care if that's trite!) Carol kicks me—an I-told-you-so kick.

"Now, Sam," Mr. Calhoun says, "let's hear from you. Please use *trite* in a sentence."

"My sandwich was trite." Sam grins as a couple of kids burst out laughing. Carol scribbles "Bozo" underneath her doodling.

"Amusing, but wrong." Mr. Calhoun hasn't smiled.

"But she said stale." Sam points to me. Mr. Calhoun says he's still waiting to hear somebody use *trite* correctly in a sentence. I slump down next to Carol, praying he won't call on me again.

That night I ask Mom, "What's wrong with Mr. Calhoun?"

Startled, Mom puts her arm around me. "Back up, Lizzie. What happened? Are you in some sort of trouble at school?"

When I shake my head, Mom relaxes. "Then what's bothering you?"

I'm not sure how to explain it. "We knew he was going to be strict," I begin, "and we'd heard all these things about how strange he is . . ." Watching Mom frown, I decide not to mention what Carol and Gloria said. "He just isn't friendly, like most teachers."

"Didn't Norman have him?" Mom asks. "I don't remember complaints."

"That's because Norman was the teacher's pet! That's part of my problem."

Mom shakes her head. "It shouldn't be. You're just as good a student as Norman, Lizzie."

"Mr. Calhoun says that, too." I report his comments on me (but not Doug's and Sam's).

"Not the best choice of words," Mom agrees, "but he

meant to compliment you. It probably won't be the only time a teacher compares you to your brother. If that's all, you shouldn't worry." Mom gives me a hug. "Feeling better now?"

When I nod, she goes to start supper. I go to the window seat and strum my fingers on the typewriter case. *Clickclickclickclick.*

He has favorites in class and he isn't fair. As I start to type these words, I know that's what's wrong.

It isn't the rumors about him. And it isn't the kids teasing me.

I type out what Mr. Calhoun said to Carol and Doug and Sam. When they made mistakes, he made them look stupid. And he made it worse by the way he praised me.

I slip out to meet Norman bringing Winston back from a walk.

"Norman, tell me something. When you had Mr. Calhoun—"

"Great guy," says Norman.

"But was he mean?" I ask. "To some kids and not to others?"

Norman nods. "He gave Chip a hard time in the beginning. Chip tried stuff like 'the dog ate my homework.' Calhoun made Chip a badge in the shape of two dog bones. They were crossed like an X, and Calhoun stamped

LAZY in the middle. He told Chip to wear it until he got his homework in—or came up with a better line!"

Maybe my class got off easy.

"You have to prove yourself with Calhoun," Norman goes on. "You can't coast in his class."

"He told us that. Then what?"

"We had a great year. He knows his stuff. He was my favorite teacher."

"What if you're not his favorite student?" I ask.

"Lizzie, did you blow it already?" Norman shakes his head. "After I paved the way . . . well, you'll pull through."

I don't say a word about Carol. "How did Chip do it?"

Norman scratches Winston's ears. "Oh, Chip wasn't in the doghouse too long. Once he got serious about math, Calhoun was impressed. The LAZY-bones badge got pinned on somebody else." Norman points a finger at me. "So you should do the extra-credit problems, Lizzie. You'll get bonus points. I can help you."

"Thanks, Norman." I have to laugh. "I'll be fine in math."

After supper I call Carol. I'm hoping what Norman told me will make her feel better. Mr. Calhoun doesn't bear grudges. After a bumpy start his classes are fun.

"It helps if you do the extra-credit math problems," I tell her.

"Boy, that sounds fun," Carol groans. "Now I've got some news for you. He's *not* from Australia. Or England. He was born on a farm, out west. In Canada! He was orphaned—that's the terrible thing that happened. Then he was sent off to boarding school, where the teachers were all super-strict. Lizzie, you there? That's why he's so . . ."

Oh, brother. I don't want to hear any more stories. Maybe, instead, I'll let the school year speak for itself.

If Lizziewhizzie EVER catches on, I'm changing my name!

DOG DAYS
* * *

October

If you don't like dogs, don't read this story!

For her third birthday, Ellie wants a puppy. Mom says no.

"We have Winston," Mom says. "One dog in the family is enough."

Mom whistles, and Winston bounds into the room. "Here, Ellie," Mom says. "Winston is your dog, too. Come play."

Winston runs to me instead. I scratch his ears and give Mom a shrug. Ellie stretches her arms toward Winston and howls. I ignore her.

"Lizzie," Mom says sharply, "you're not acting like a big girl."

"But, Mom." I follow her to the sewing room. "Ellie treats Winston like a baby. It's not my fault if he doesn't like it."

Mom picks up my Halloween costume, which so far consists of a trench coat of Norman's. (I'm going to be a secret agent.)

"Winston likes attention," Mom says, glancing over her shoulder. "Look at him now. He's happy as can be, romping around with your sister."

I frown. "Why can't we get her a puppy of her own?"

"Out of the question," says Mom, lifting me to a chair so she can pin up the hem of Norman's coat. "Too much work."

"Not if Ellie takes care of it," I suggest.

Mom shakes her head. "That's not realistic, Lizzie." *Clickclickclick*. I hear footsteps (and paw steps) close by. My costume comes off—no way will I let Ellie see it. No smart secret agent would take such a chance!

Over the weekend, Carol phones me. "Lizzie, he's done it again."

"Who? What?"

"Drew, that's who. The big baby always gets his way. So guess what he got."

"Tell me."

"A dog! A mutt, to be exact!" Carol wails, "If only my mom had listened to me. Brownie is going to be such a pain."

"Is Brownie a puppy?" I ask, trying not to sound jealous.

"Yeah," Carol says. "She's not trained yet, if you know what I mean."

I laugh. "You'll get used to that part." Then I invite her to bring Brownie over. I can't wait to tell Ellie a puppy is coming to visit.

But Ellie is out with Mom running some errands. Mom left a note asking Norman and me to rake leaves while they're gone.

For a half hour, Norman and I work together. We rake the leaves into two mounds, each standing two feet tall. Except for the clear patch of ground between our piles, leaves cover our yard all the way to the creek.

Where's Carol? I wonder. Then I hear Winston barking; it must be at Brownie!

Rats. It's the sheepdog—and Chip.

Norman announces he's taking a break. He whistles for Winston. Chip tosses a football to Norman, while the dogs romp in the unraked leaves. *Clackclackclack Crunch.*

I work for a few more minutes, before tossing the rake aside. I'm not doing the whole yard by myself. Norman throws a wild pass, and the football hits my arm. Rubbing the sore spot, I scowl at Norman. Instead of going off to play, he could have asked Chip to help us bag and rake.

Just then a small brownish dog tugs Carol into our yard.

Carol jerks the leash. "Stop already! We're here!"

"What took you so long?" I ask.

"Drew." Carol rolls her eyes. "Threw a fit. You don't want to know." She hands me the leash. "He won't let Brownie out of his sight, unless there's 'dog work' to be done. I had to bribe him with a Nestlé Crunch—or he would have come, too!"

I kneel beside Brownie. She's part dachshund, maybe, since her body is shaped like a sausage. She sniffs, then licks my knee.

Carol says, "When do they stop that?"

"Stop what?"

"Licking people. It's disgusting."

"They don't. Stop licking, I mean. It's their way of exploring."

Carol sighs. "I was hoping Brownie would outgrow it. Your dog doesn't go around licking everybody, does he?"

"Not everybody. He sniffs a lot, though." Maybe this wasn't the greatest idea, to have Carol come over. I'm surprised she seems so uncomfortable around dogs. I can't help thinking about Ellie—she'd go nuts over Brownie. My sister wants a dog she can't have while my best friend has a dog she doesn't want. No fair!

I unhook Brownie's leash and give her a ride on my shoulders. She's so light, compared to Winston. I can't remember him ever being that small!

The minute I put Brownie down, she drools on Carol's

leg. Carol stamps her foot, making it worse. I hand her some leaves to wipe the stuff off.

We take a slow tour of the yard. We talk about Halloween costumes (Carol's will be Cleopatra) and about Mr. Calhoun (who lets us call him "Mr. C."). Every week he seems friendlier. For once, Norman was right.

We even talk about Doug and Sam—and agree that Doug's the "bigger bozo." We agree on everything, in fact. Except dogs.

"Liddie!" Ellie is back, sooner than I expected. From the back door Mom waves to me and points out Ellie. It's her signal that I'm on baby-duty. "Why now?" I grumble, though I know Mom can't hear me.

Turning to Ellie, I say, "My name is Liz-zie. With two z's and no d's. You could *try* to get it right."

But Ellie is much more interested in Brownie. "Puppy doggie!" she squeals as Brownie runs in zigzags, chasing a squirrel toward a tree.

"Here, Brownie! Meet Ellie," I call out, but the puppy has her own ideas. She's off to the creek, after Winston. Ellie tries to run after them.

I pull her back. "It's muddy down there. Okay for dogs, not for you."

"Muddy?" Carol snaps. "If I have to give that mutt a bath—"

"Mutt?" Ellie tugs at my sleeve. "Muddy mutt?"

"The puppy's name is Brownie," I say with a nudge to Carol. "Watch what you say or it'll stick."

Carol points to the sheepdog. "Whose dog is that?"

"Not ours, thank goodness!" I point to Chip. "He looks like his dog, don't you think?"

Near the creek Winston is playing with Brownie. The sheepdog runs toward us; he must be feeling left out.

"Go away!" Carol shouts. "I don't want to be licked!" She flings a stick over the sheepdog's head. He streaks off into the leaves. *Clicketyclicketylickety-split!*

Uh-oh. The stick lands beside one of the piles of raked leaves. "Don't go there!" I call to the sheepdog, but he won't stop for me. Leaves scatter every which way as he plows through the pile.

I rush around the remains of the mound. The sheepdog charges out, shedding leaves as he runs. "Bad dog," I shout. But through the same passage come Winston and Brownie. Winston stops when he sees me, shaking leaves off his nose.

"Winston," I cry, "raking leaves is hard work!" Winston paws the ground. I reach down to rub his fur.

I look up for a moment. Brownie sniffs Ellie. In a flash, though, they're gone!

"Come back!" I yell. But they're off, racing toward

Carol. Ellie, Brownie, and the sheepdog, who still has that stupid stick in his mouth.

Right in their path is the other mound of raked leaves.

I wave wildly to Carol. "Stop that dog! Move!" But she's busy examining the sole of her shoe—she must have stepped in something. She doesn't even look up until the last minute, when she hears Brownie bark.

"Stop, doggie!" Ellie shouts. And the sheepdog does, just in front of the leaf pile. Ellie runs around him, waving her arms like a windmill. The sheepdog drops the stick at Ellie's feet.

Before I can get there, Ellie does just what I hoped she would do. She tosses the stick at me—away from the leaf pile. The sheepdog is off and running again!

"Nice job," I tell Ellie as we move away from the mound of raked leaves. "You just saved us a whole lot of work."

I glance over my shoulder at Norman and Chip, who are playing football. "You could watch your own dog," I growl at Chip. (He can't hear me, but he fumbles the next catch, I'm happy to say.)

We walk toward Carol, with Brownie sniffing our heels. Ellie stops often to pet her. "Doggie kiss!" she says, laughing when Brownie licks her hand.

Carol is busy wiping her shoe with a stick. "Look at

this . . . mess you made," she scolds Brownie, tossing the stick aside. "I wish we could take you back to the pound."

"Carol, don't say that!" I shout.

"Pound?" Ellie tugs my hand.

"You don't want to know." I pull Ellie closer. "Really, Carol. You're lucky to have Brownie. You're just not used to her yet. But we can help you." I turn to Ellie, who swings my arm back and forth. "We'll help Carol with her puppy. Won't that be fun?"

"Puppy funny." Ellie beams.

"Very. Too bad I can't leave her with you." Carol looks up at Ellie. "Dogs like you, I can tell. You're much better with Brownie than my little brother is." She shakes her head. "Between him and me it'll take a miracle to get that mutt trained!"

Ruffruffruffruffruff. Winston is barking much faster than normal.

I run toward the creek to meet him halfway. "What's wrong?" I cry.

Ruffruffruff . . . "Ugh!" I shout. I turn, holding my nose as I point to Winston. "Carol, Ellie, stay back," I try warning them. But Ellie skips over, with Brownie sniffing her ankles. Carol walks with her head down, kicking at leaves.

"Ellie," I call out, "don't come closer. And keep Brownie away from Winston!"

Ellie sniffs. "Funny smell."

"Hold your nose," I tell her. "I think it's a—"

The sheepdog charges over to Winston just as Carol shows up.

"Yikes!" she screams. "Did a stink bomb go off around here?"

"Skunk." One whiff of the sheepdog proves that. He smells like he fell in a sewer! He must have taken the hit: Compared to him, Winston smells like a daisy. (A stinky daisy.)

"Barf!" says Carol. "We better get out of here." Ellie helps her fasten Brownie's leash. I shout to Norman and Chip to come over.

"You're lucky," I tell Carol. "Brownie's okay."

I shake my head at Winston. "Sorry, boy, but you're in for a major bath."

I hear Norman and Chip whistling to the dogs. Suddenly they stop; Chip sticks his nose in his sleeve. "Lizzie," shouts Norman, "what have you done to them?"

"Me?" I shout back. "Nothing!"

"They stink!" Chip says—as if he's breaking the news.

"They ran into a skunk. While you guys were playing, that is."

We argue about who should have been watching, and who's going to have to clean up the dogs. "I hear a tomato juice bath gets rid of the smell," Norman says with a glance at Carol.

"What are you looking at me for?" Carol says. "I don't need tomato juice. Brownie didn't go near the skunk."

Norman glares back. "Bully for you and Brownie. Is *that* your dog's name?"

Chip says, "It looks more like a hot dog than a brownie."

"So do you," Carol says.

Chip's face turns as red as tomato juice. His fingers twitch. "Stupid runt," he mutters to Norman. "Got 'em skunked, I bet."

I feel like screaming "It's all *your* dog's fault!" I nudge Carol, who yanks Brownie's leash. "Let's go," I say.

"Dogs are such trouble," Carol says as Brownie pulls her toward the gate. "As if cleaning up after their you-know-what isn't bad enough, I have skunks to worry about—" Suddenly Carol stretches to see over my shoulder. "Lizzie, look at your sister."

Across the yard Ellie is giving Winston a great big hug. Then the sheepdog shuffles over, and she pets him, too! I should run and pull her away, but it's too late for that. I lean on the gate, watching and shaking my head.

"How can she stand it?" asks Carol. "The stink, I mean."

"She doesn't care," I say. "She loves dogs."

"No kidding," Carol says. "Better stock up on tomato juice."

Now I don't really mind about Ellie playing with Winston. I know Winston wants her to. His ears stick up like triangles whenever he sees her. Even after taking turns in bathtubs full of tomato juice, Ellie and Winston are the best of friends. For once, I guess, I don't mind her copying. She learned to love dogs from me!

Now, how about Carol?

SAVING FOR SKATES
* * *

Who says $$$$$ doesn't grow on trees?

I'm learning to skate. Compared to swimming, it's easy! I can glide across the ice, forward and backwards. I can do crossovers—one foot in front of the other—most of the time. But I wish I had skates of my own.

If I had new skates, they would fit me better than the ones we rent. My ankles wouldn't wobble. People would point and say, "Look at Lizzie. Isn't she graceful?" Then I'd trace a perfect figure eight with my shiny new blades.

"Mom," I hint, "if you're wondering what to get for my birthday, my *tenth* birthday, coming soon . . ." Across the kitchen floor I glide toward her and spin right into her arms!

"Wish I could," says Mom, shaking her head. "But ice

skates cost more than I can spend on a birthday present right now. We need new winter boots, since you've all outgrown last year's—"

"Please," I groan, "don't buy me boots for my birthday!"

She smiles. "All I meant was you'll outgrow your skates, too, if we buy them now."

"What if I use my own money?"

"Lizzie," Norman butts in, "are you deaf? Mom said no. You know what skates cost? Too much! Money doesn't grow on trees."

"Rats," I say. "There goes that idea."

"A new pair of skates costs one hundred and twenty dollars," Norman goes on. "If you save all of your allowance, it will take you over two *years* to have enough money."

I frown. I can do the math—and my allowance is one dollar a week. If I want to buy skates, I have to earn the money some other way. Yard work for the neighbors? I'm sick of raking leaves! A bake sale? I don't know enough recipes or cook well enough, I'm afraid.

Then the idea comes to me—I have *stuff* I could sell. I'll have a yard sale. Under the trees, I'll rake in cash instead of leaves! Won't you-know-who be surprised?

"Listen," I sound out Ellie. "I have a plan to make lots of money. We can sell old toys and games we don't play with anymore. You know, stuff like this sailboat puzzle. It has only six pieces, and it's way too easy. But . . ." Ellie grabs the puzzle away from me and dumps it on the floor. "I'm going to need your help."

Mom likes my idea. Ellie follows us around as we search the house. Ellie hides Lulu and her beanbag monkey in her bed. "Don't be silly," I say. "I wouldn't dream of selling those."

In my closet I find two sets of Chinese checkers. "Let's sell both. I never liked this game."

"My game." Ellie reaches for both boxes.

"Ellie," I groan. "We need things to sell." But Mom puts one set back in our closet.

I think about new skates each time I see an old toy. Soon our room is full of piles: jump ropes, squirt guns, pop beads, jigsaw puzzles. A clown puppet with strings to move the arms and legs. A ball Winston used to play with. (He won't mind.) Two Barbie dolls. A doll buggy full of stuffed animals.

"Are you sure you want to sell so many animals?" Mom cuddles a floppy puppy. "This one is cute."

"Oh, Mom, they're for babies. I'd rather play with Winston than some silly toy dog."

"Me, too," says Ellie. (And she *does*.)

Mom places the puppy back in the buggy. I give it a shove toward the hall. "All you guys are for sale."

* * *

I make signs out of cardboard, writing in big letters with different-colored markers:

YARD SALE

SATURDAY AT NOON

FEATURING TOYS, GAMES, PUZZLES

GREAT BARGINS!

Norman looks over my shoulder. "Can't you spell?" In the middle of my last word he writes a big A in his crummy handwriting.

"You messed up my sign."

He doesn't apologize. "So what's this about?"

"I'm going to raise lots and lots of money, right there." I point to the yard. "Maybe money *does* grow on trees!"

"Ha ha. Lizzie, you're such a wit." (Norman makes it sound like "twit.") "Tell you what. I have a few things to sell, too. Things that lots of kids would want."

"What kind of things?" I chew on a braid. Where's the catch?

"Come on. This is a good deal for you. A bigger sale will bring in more customers. I'll keep the money from any of my stuff that gets sold. The rest is yours."

On Saturday the first thing Norman brings outside is a World Series poster. It's a picture of a lot of men all lined up wearing baseball uniforms. The edges are crumpled. One corner is held together with tape. No one besides Norman would want it.

Norman puts the poster right in the middle of our picnic table. I try turning the picture sideways, to make room for my jump ropes and the box of Chinese checkers.

"Keep your paws off my poster!" Norman shoves it back to the middle of the table. "Nobody will want it with your fingerprints on it!"

"Nobody will want it anyway," I say. "You got it for free by sending in Wheaties box tops. Who'd want to pay you for it?"

"It's historic." Norman writes "$10" on the poster's price tag. "You just watch. It will be the first thing to go."

A little girl from the next block arrives right at noon. "Look!" she cries out. "Barbie dolls, for only two dollars each!"

But Ellie reaches the Barbies first. She takes them off the table before the other girl can buy anything.

"Hey, bring those back!" I yell. Too late. The Barbies and Ellie are gone.

Marvin, from my swimming class, picks up Norman's goggles. Their price is five dollars.

"Wow!" Marvin slips the goggles over his nose. The strap breaks.

"Fifty cents," Marvin offers.

"No way," says Norman.

While they argue, Winston runs up. He stops to sniff Marvin's feet.

"Nice dog," says Marvin.

I hug Winston, hoping nobody thinks *he's* for sale. New customers arrive. Some friends of Norman's spend a lot of time looking at his World Series poster. Nobody buys it.

"So where's your dorky friend and her dopey dog?" Norman asks.

"Carol's busy today." (I don't mention she's taking Brownie to obedience school.) "And don't call my friend names."

"She called my friend a hot dog," says Norman.

"He insulted her first."

"No, he didn't."

"Did too." I walk off before he can get the last word in this argument.

We have customers in our yard all afternoon. But some of the kids don't buy anything, or haven't brought much money along. I try cutting the price of the Chinese checkers game to one dollar, but it still doesn't sell. The stuffed animals aren't selling, either. I spot the floppy puppy Mom liked and put it aside. I'll save it for her, as an extra Christmas present. I think about saving the Chinese checkers for Ellie, until I remember we have another set in the closet already.

The Barbies are still gone from the table. For a moment I hope they've been sold.

No such luck. They're off with Ellie, being smothered with hugs.

"Ellie, look." I sit down with her. "Those Barbies were mine. But how about one for you and one for me? You can pick the one you like best."

I hold out my hand. "Deal?"

"Deal!" says Ellie.

After she chooses, I put the other doll back on the table. Right on top of Norman's poster.

"Oh, she has glitter in her hair!" The girl from the next block is back, pulling her mother toward the table. "She's the Barbie I've always wanted."

When the girl's mother offers me five dollars for the doll, I give her the poster, too.

I count up the money from the sale. Altogether, we have $48.50. Ten dollars is Norman's share. The rest is mine.

"Good job, Lizzie," Mom says.

"Not bad," says Norman. "We could have made more money on that poster, but, hey, I'm not complaining."

I won't complain, either, but we didn't raise as much as I'd hoped.

"I don't have enough for skates," I say. "Not for new ones, that is."

Mom picks up Ellie, who's poking her with the Barbie doll. "We could look at used skates."

"Maybe," I said. "But I want them to fit me. The rental skates are used, and they don't." Winston curls up at my feet and falls asleep. Suddenly, I'm tired, too.

"I have used skates, and they're fine," Norman says. "The trick is . . ." He breaks off, laughing. "Shall I tell you my secret?"

This better be good. "Okay, Norman, what is it?"

"Learn to skate! You won't wobble around, unless you can't skate to begin with!" He winks. "And if your skates feel big, wear thicker socks."

"Lizzie," Mom says, "would you like to take lessons? I'll pay for them. Or I'll help you buy new skates, if that's still what you want. Not right away, but with your money and my share and the birthday check from your father, we should have enough in a couple of months."

I shut my eyes. I see myself on the ice gliding forward, then backwards, then twirling into a spin. I don't want to wait a couple of months—half the winter will be over!

"Sign me up," I say. "*Advanced* beginners."

With my yard sale earnings we buy a pair of used skates from the rink. We find thick socks in jazzy colors at a ski shop; I choose royal blue with hot pink and black stripes.

The blades of my skates aren't shiny, and the white leather is scuffed at the heels. But the skates fit (for now). I can't wait for my lessons to start.

My feet are still growing, though. Faster than ever.

Norman catches me measuring them with a ruler. "What's the matter? One foot bigger than the other?"

"I'm doing a math problem," I mumble, hoping to get rid of him.

"Ha." Norman points to my skates with the ruler. "So what's the problem? Your feet got too big?"

"My feet are fine, Norman. So are my skates." I rub the leather. Just a few creases. *Almost* new. Pretty soon I'll be putting in creases and scuff marks of my own.

"Don't worry," he says. "When you outgrow those, you can always have another yard sale."

Another yard sale? Easy for him to say!

SECRET SANTA
* * *

DECEMBER

You can't fool me!

"Lizzie, who'd you get?" Carol asks on our way out of school.

I stall, hoping she'll forget her question. In class today we drew names for "Secret Santa." Mr. Calhoun gave us his rules for this game: *Don't tell* is the most important rule of all.

"I'll tell you if you tell me," Carol says. "Nobody else will know."

Huh? Even if I wanted to tell her, which I don't, I wouldn't announce it here in the school yard.

Instead of answering, I offer Carol a Life Saver. "Okay, let me guess." Carol picks red, even though a yellow one was on top. "You got—"

"I'm not telling, so stop trying to worm it out of me."

Carol kicks a pebble. "I thought we were best friends."

"We are." I make a sour face, because she left me the lemon Life Saver. "But I'm still not telling."

During the next three weeks, we're supposed to leave clues for the person whose name we picked. "Be creative. Mysterious, baffling," Mr. Calhoun had said, giving a wink, since *baffling* is on our vocabulary list. "Write notes with invisible ink or use cutouts from newspapers and magazines. Find a messenger to deliver them, so you can be *anonymous*." (Another vocabulary word.) "And remember, one of your classmates drew your name and will be trying to outwit you."

On the last day of school before Christmas, each of us brings a present for the person whose name we picked. We'll open our presents, then guess who our "Secret Santa" was.

"Glad tidings," said Mr. Calhoun, tossing his own name into the pile. "The more of you fooled, the merrier. But I warn you—I always guess right. You can't fool me!"

"Have it your way," Carol grumbles. "It would have been fun to work on the hints together. But I don't care. I've got lots of ideas, more than I need for—" She bites her lip. "But if you must do it on your own, it's okay."

It isn't. She's going to be sore at me. But after she almost blurts out the name she drew, I *can't* tell her mine. I dig into my pocket for the scrap of paper—with the name of the person who can't be fooled. To break that streak, I have to work alone—in "top secret" mode.

I can't wait to leave my first clue. Since he knows my handwriting, I'll *type* my messages. I slip a piece of red construction paper into the typewriter:

To Mr. C. from S.S. Here is your first hint.
My name sounds silly in Pig Latin.

I read it out loud. Baffling, all right! I can see Mr. C. adjusting his eyeglasses, searching my words for some hidden meaning. The clue could come from anyone. And since everybody seems to know Pig Latin, it doesn't rule anybody out.

"Talking to yourself, Lizzie?" Help! It's Norman.

I clap my hand over the message.

"So," says Norman, "let me guess. You got the booby prize. You're the Secret Santa for Mr. Calhoun!"

Shocked, I stare up at Norman. My fingers slip off the paper.

"Lizzie, give me credit. I had the guy for fifth grade. It's that time of year." How did he manage to read my mind?

I slump into the corner of the window seat. The secret

is out, right off the bat. Why did I bother to keep it from Carol?

Norman pulls over a chair. "Want some help from a pro?"

Norman will "help" whether I want him to or not. "In your class," I ask, "who was Mr. Calhoun's Secret Santa?"

"Uh, um." Norman blushes. "It was Gloria."

This sounds interesting. "What were her clues?"

Norman shrugs. "Who knows? She blabbed to her friends that she had the teacher. He didn't need other clues."

"Is my clue weird?" I roll the paper out of the typewriter.

Norman grins. "It looks impossible."

I guess that's a compliment.

Before the first week is over, I learn Carol has Sam. She lets it slip out in the lunch line, the day I forgot my sandwich and had to buy. I bet everyone around us, including the serving lady, overheard. Too bad Carol and I weren't speaking in code then!

Carol isn't worried. "Sam's over there, at the bozos' table." She points across the cafeteria. "Anyway, I can throw him off the trail."

"How?" I try poking the fish sticks. My fork gets stuck. Some green stuff (spinach?) runs into the mashed potatoes. I try pushing it aside with a spoon.

"For my second clue, I'm going to say I like dogs. And ice-skating."

I stop stirring the mashed potatoes. "But that's not true. You don't skate or like dogs."

"Sure I do, if I'm you." Carol grins.

"Isn't that against the rules? You can't pretend to be me—that's unfair." My spoon clatters against the plate.

"Sure it's fair," Carol says loudly. "Go ask Mr. Calhoun. He never said we couldn't."

Be creative. Mysterious. Baffling. Carol looks proud of herself. I wonder if that was her idea all along, that we pretend to be each other.

I glare at what's left on my plate. Everything. Even Carol didn't bother with the fish sticks or the green stuff. Since she finished her potatoes, I let her have mine.

That night, I type my next clue on green construction paper.

> Mr. C., Here's your second hint about my
> name. If you see double <u>double</u>, you're on
> the right track.

LIZZIE has two sets of double letters, but I don't think he'll figure this out. He still calls me Elizabeth in class.

Meanwhile, from *my* Secret Santa—zip. No messages,

nothing! It's no fair if nobody leaves me clues. I try to remember if anybody was absent the day we drew names and wonder if I should tell Mr. C. I've been left out.

At the end of the second week, a bulgy envelope shows up in my locker. When I rip open the envelope, cutout letters fall on the floor. My "Santa" must have run out of glue.

Some clue. I stuff the pieces back in—I won't have time to unscramble the letters at school. Before gym class I corner Carol to see if she made the "delivery."

"Don't try to worm it out of me," she says, and walks ahead of me into the gym. Still sore, I guess.

The next day Norman says, "Hey, Lizzie. What's your present for the Big Calhoun-a?"

"I don't know yet." I'm at the kitchen counter, flipping through a cookbook. "What did Gloria give him?"

"An apple."

"Really? That's such an ordinary idea."

Norman shrugs. "Maybe it was a chocolate apple." He peers over my shoulder at the cookbook. "Dog biscuits! Now *that's* a great idea."

"That's my present for Winston—"

"Make an extra batch. Lizzie, you're a genius!" Norman claps me on the back. "What have we here?" He mimicks

Mr. C.'s voice. "Christmas cookies? A bit oddly shaped . . . could this be a bone?" Norman almost chokes with laughter.

"Norman," I say, "I'm not giving Mr. Calhoun dog biscuits." I sound as if I'm talking to Ellie. "You want me to flunk?"

"Lighten up, Lizzie. Calhoun can take a joke."

"Easy for you to say." I close the cookbook with a bang.

Still laughing, Norman leaves the room. But now, when I think about presents for my teacher, my mind goes blank. I could bring him red pencils or chalk or a big box of paper clips. But those sound duller than Gloria's apple!

I wish I'd picked somebody else. If only I had Carol. For her present, I'd make a friendship bracelet—or a hair band. I'd use glitter glue on the messages, and I'd write the clues in calligraphy with a quill pen.

For Mr. Calhoun? I open the cookbook again. What about . . . gingerbread? Here's a recipe for gingerbread men—two dozen will be perfect. I'll make twelve of them boys and eleven girls, just like our class. And the tallest one will have eyeglasses, just like him!

For my last clue, I type on a paper napkin:

Mr. C., This is your final hint. Some
people get my name wrong, and I bet you
will, too. I hope you like your present.

He won't know about Michele and Liddie and Lizziewhizzie (not to mention Lizard). If he isn't baffled by this clue, I give up!

On the last day of school before Christmas, Mr. Calhoun surprises us with a pizza party. Instead of lunch period in the cafeteria, we get to eat pizza in his classroom. Hooray!

At lunch Sam sits down across the aisle from me, instead of his usual place in the back. Finally, he leans over to ask, "Do you have a dog?"

"Yeah. Why?" As if I don't know!

He's blushing. "Oh, I just wondered . . . what's your dog's name?"

"Winston." I glance over my shoulder at Carol at the pizza table. Was *he* a clue, too?

"Thought so," Sam says, smiling. I smile back.

After lunch our game begins. Mr. Calhoun, in a Santa Claus hat, distributes the packages. With his white hair poking out, he looks almost jolly. It's hard to imagine we ever thought he was mean.

One by one, we open our presents—and guess.

Sam guesses me. "Sorry," I say. Sam's mouth drops open. His present was a deck of cards with pictures of dogs on the backs. He can't believe he's wrong.

On the next kid's turn, I sneak a look at Carol. She

sticks up her thumb. I hope Mr. C. didn't see her, since she's not supposed to reveal whose name she got until everyone else has guessed.

I have no idea who has me. My first—and only—message was hopeless: eighty-seven letters all jumbled up. If any had stuck to the page, I might have cracked the code. But it felt like I'd been given Humpty Dumpty to put back together again. The only word I managed to find in that mess was my own name.

I keep track of the names that were guessed. So far, six kids guessed right. Those "Santas" can't be mine. Soon it's Carol's turn. When she opens her present, she glows.

"I knew it!" She slips a friendship bracelet around her wrist, waves her arm in the air. "It has to be Lizzie!"

"It's not." My voice catches. Carol looks crushed. I see a girl named Maureen sticking her thumb in the air. *It's only a game,* I want to say. But Mr. Calhoun is handing a package to me.

Inside are six letters—rubber stamps that spell LIZZIE. "Thanks!" I call out. The stamps will be really fun to use.

Now I have to guess. A girl, I bet. I eliminate Carol and Maureen and the three other girls who were guessed already. Not counting me, that leaves five. Eeny meeny miny mo . . .

"Time's up," says Mr. Calhoun.

I guess wildly, "Sandra."

"That's right!" Sandra Conti, the short girl in the front row, seems pleased that I guessed her. She's new—just moved here this fall from Chicago.

"These are great." I show the stamps to the class. (Maybe sometime I'll ask Sandra to translate her clue.)

A minute later Doug guesses Sandra on his turn, too! It figures—he can't remember a thing!

Mr. Calhoun goes last. I know he's kept track of the guesses. Still, I bet he's fooled. My clues gave nothing about me away.

"Gingerbread cookies. My favorites. Thank you, Secret Santa."

Carol raises her hand. "Do you know who it is?"

"I think so," says Mr. Calhoun.

Two boys shout, "Guess! Guess!" Mr. Calhoun calls for quiet.

I fiddle with my rubber stamps, rearranging the letters to spell ZILIEZ, pretending I'm not a bit interested in what he'll say.

"Now, this wasn't easy," Mr. Calhoun goes on. "But I noticed one thing on all three clues that makes me sure. My Secret Santa is . . . Elizabeth Anderson!"

"You mean Lizzie," somebody shouts. "She's been guessed already."

Sam and Carol chime in, "But our guesses were wrong."

"You're right," I tell Mr. Calhoun.

"Nice try, *Lizzie*." He bites into a cookie. "These are perfect."

"So, Lizzie," Norman says after school. "You pull one over on Calhoun?"

"He guessed me." I'm at the typewriter, punching the keys.

"How?" Norman sounds surprised. "Your clues were tough."

I nod. "But I made one big goof. I typed them. He could tell they didn't come from a computer. It's your fault, too."

"How come?"

"He remembered Mom because he taught you. He remembered she works for a newspaper, and he figured we might still have a typewriter at home."

"Smart guy," says Norman. "Nobody's fooled him yet."

"Guess not." I type **Mr. C. gets an A.** *Click.*

"Well," Norman says, "if you'd listened to me—"

"And given him dog biscuits?" I shake my head. "No way."

A little later I telephone Carol.

"Hello, Elizabeth."

"Who, me or my great-aunt?" My joke falls flat. Five seconds tick by.

"Listen, you didn't have to fool *me*."

"I didn't try to."

"I mean, you wouldn't tell me a thing, after I begged you to tell. So then it hits me—you must have my name. How could I know that Maureen would try to copy *you*? You should have seen the clues I got, in that glittery kind of ink you like to use." Carol sighs. "I wanted it to be true, that my best friend and my Secret Santa were the same person. And I don't like to be fooled."

"I'm sorry," I say, not because I fooled her, but because she feels so bad. "It's only a game. You fooled Sam."

"He's a bozo," Carol snaps. "It hardly counts."

"Sam's not so bad," I say, remembering his smile. "Anyway, the rest of us weren't the greatest players, except for Mr. Calhoun. Isn't it funny how he always guesses right?"

Silence. She's sulking, so I say, "You know what my brother told me to do? For the present? Dog biscuits. Really and truly. I was going to bake some for Winston, and Norman told me to give a batch to Mr. Calhoun."

Carol laughs, then stops short. "How could you tell Norman you were Mr. Calhoun's Secret Santa and not tell me?"

"Oh, Carol, I didn't tell. Norman snooped!"

"I could have told you he would," she sniffs.

I invite her over. Cooking might cheer her up. "I still want to make dog biscuits, for Winston's Christmas present. You can take some home to Brownie."

"Sure, Lizzie," she says, and sounds pleased. "But let's not keep secrets from each other, okay?"

"Okay. Let's tell each other *everything*," I add.

"Promise?"

"Promise."

"Starting now?"

"This minute." I wish she could see my grin. "So, Carol." I almost burst out laughing. "What are you getting me for my birthday?"

Or give me a hint!

BY LIZZIE

* * *

On December 30, Norman tricks me.

I'm at the typewriter, in the window seat. **What are you getting me for my birthday? Or give me a hint!** *Click-clickety, clack clack, click-clack!* I roll out the last page and clip all my stories together. I'm done, just in time.

Tomorrow's the big day—the "Big 1-0," Norman calls it. I'm in the best mood. When Norman slinks over, dropping Winston's leash in my lap, I'm happy to take our dog for a walk. Especially when Norman says he'll shovel the snow and wrap all my presents while we're out.

Once we're gone, he reads the whole thing! He's lounging by the typewriter, reading the last page, when Winston and I rush in from outside. Forgetting his training, Winston jumps right over the doormat and shakes snow on the living-room floor. Ellie runs up to us, wearing her hair in a ponytail. (I'm sticking with braids.) She's also wearing her new red-and-white checked dress and a Santa Claus hat.

"That's mine!" I scream—and I *don't* mean the dress! Norman holds my pages just out of reach. "Norman!"

"I know, I should have asked. But stop yelping. It's a masterpiece."

"You like it?" You never can tell with Norman.

"You made up a lot of good stuff. Very clever, Lizzie."

I roll my eyes. "You don't know what you're talking about."

Norman waves a few pages in the air. "Come on. We did *not* sell my World Series poster along with some Barbie doll for five dollars! I did *not* tell you to bake dog biscuits for your teacher—that crazy idea was all yours! We *don't* have skunks in our yard, unless you count your friend the dork. And what swimming group are you in? Aren't you still a beginner?"

"Shows what you know," I say.

"And the time that dork called me up? What a joke. Ha ha. If you think for one minute you fooled me—"

"Did too, Norman. And it *is* funny. At the time, I didn't think so. But now, when I see what I've written, I can laugh."

"Well, I know what *really* happened." Norman hands over my stories. "I should write a book."

Winston barks. Ellie pounds at the typewriter. "Me, too, Lissie." (Almost!)

"Tough luck, Norman," I say. "I beat you to it." I pat Ellie. "You, too. Both of you'd better be nice to me . . ." I wave some pages under Norman's nose. ". . . or I just might send in a story or two to the school magazine. So everybody can read all about you!"

"Who cares?" Norman says. "Like they'd want to publish *you*."

This time, when he stomps off, I send Ellie after him. "Go see if he's wrapping my birthday present." I slip a roll of tape in her hand. "He might need your help."

I snap the case of the typewriter closed. Touching the stickers, I think about all the places the typewriter has been. A year around the world with Mom, and now a whole year here with me. I should make a LIZZIE sticker. The rubber stamps I got from my Secret Santa, Sandra, will do a great job. I'm going to paste LIZZIE right there in the middle.

Here in my family, I'm still in the middle. But I don't feel so stuck anymore. Next year, who knows? I may write new stories. New places? Not likely. New people? You bet!

Tomorrow's the big day. Tomorrow I'll show Mom my

stories. I think she'll like them—wasn't she in the middle herself? (Not *exactly* like me, though.)

And tomorrow, I'm ten—at last.

Click click. Quiet, Winston. I'm getting the last word after all.